PAYBACK TIME

PAYBACK TIME

by

Carl Deuker

HOUGHTON MIFFLIN

HOUGHTON MIFFLIN HARCOURT

BOSTON   NEW YORK

The author
would like to thank
Ann Rider, the editor of this
book, for her advice and
encouragement.

■ ■ ■ ■

Copyright © 2010 by Carl Deuker

All rights reserved. For information about permission to reproduce selections from this book, write to Permissions, Houghton Mifflin Harcourt Publishing Company, 215 Park Avenue South, New York, New York 10003.

Houghton Mifflin is an imprint of Houghton Mifflin Harcourt Publishing Company.

www.hmhbooks.com

The text of this book is set in Lino Letter.

Library of Congress Cataloging-in-Publication Data

Deuker, Carl.

Payback time / by Carl Deuker.

p. cm.

Summary: Overweight, somewhat timid Mitch reluctantly agrees to be the sports reporter for the Lincoln High newspaper because he is determined to be a writer, but he senses a real story in Angel, a talented football player who refuses to stand out on the field—or to discuss his past.

ISBN 978-0-547-27981-7

[1. Reporters and reporting--Fiction. 2. Football—Fiction. 3. Overweight persons—Fiction. 4. Courage—Fiction. 5. Secrets—Fiction. 6. High schools—Fiction. 7. Schools—Fiction.] I. Title.

PZ7.D493Pay 2010

[Fic]—dc22   2010006779

Manufactured in the United States of America

DOC 10 9 8 7 6 5

4500311363

For Anne and Marian

PART ONE

I

I'M GOING TO BE A FAMOUS REPORTER. My name—Daniel True—will be on the front page of the *New York Times*. A huge story is waiting for me, and I'll find it—no doubt about it.

Ah, who am I kidding?

There's lots of doubt about it. Nothing but doubt.

Still, a guy can dream, can't he?

When I was little, my dad took me to see *All the President's Men* at a theater that shows old movies. I didn't follow the politics about Nixon and Watergate, but as I watched I knew I was born to be a reporter. Meeting in gritty alleyways with strangers who tell you a little bit of this and a little bit of that, taking those little bits, digging deeper, asking questions, learning more until you've got a story that shakes the world—what could be more satisfying than that?

I want to live in New York City, major in journalism at Columbia University, have my finger on the pulse of the world. But instead of being at a great college in an exciting city, I'm stuck at mediocre Abraham Lincoln High School in boring Seattle.

For the past three years I've written articles for my school newspaper, but my classmates don't think of me as Daniel True, future prize-winning reporter. To them I'm not even Danny, which is what the kids called me in grade school; or Dan, which is what my mom and dad call me now. At Lincoln, I'm *Mitch*.

That doesn't sound like a bad nickname until you hear how I got it. I'm five four and I weigh 180. Okay, 190. Okay, 200 . . . three months ago. I've got wispy blond hair and skin the color of copy paper. Girls don't chase me down the halls.

Three years ago, when I first walked through the double doors of Lincoln High, Stan Bach, a football player with a Dallas Cowboys star tattooed on his neck and a voice the size of Texas, spotted me in the lunch line. "Hey, look who's a Lincoln Mustang now," he said to his friends. "It's the *Michelin Man.*" His football buddies roared as if he were funnier than the Three Stooges. *Michelin Man! Michelin Man!*

For a few weeks kids called me Michelin Man. That was shortened to Mitch Man, which got shortened to Mitch, which stuck. Now, most kids don't even know that my real name is Daniel. Sometimes even I forget.

4

Last year Ms. Bergstrom, my English teacher, kept me after class one day. "I heard how you got your nickname," she said as she roamed the room picking pencils off the floor, "and I know how much it must hurt your feelings. Always remember that Alexander Pope, one of the greatest writers of all time, was a dwarf with pockmarked skin and bad breath."

She was trying to be nice—but give me a break, lady. I'm not a zitty dwarf with halitosis. Still, after school that day I bought a large tube of Clearasil and a larger bottle of Listerine, both of which I use daily. I don't want to be "Stinky Mitch" or "Mitch the Zit."

2

LINCOLN HIGH WASN'T ALWAYS the most boring school in the world. For one incredible week, my corner of Seattle was the center of the media universe. CNN, CBS, ABC, Fox, MSNBC, the *New York Times*—you name it, and their correspondents were crawling all over Lincoln High.

It happened like this. Chance Taylor, a Lincoln senior with no mother and a drunk for a father, got involved with some Al Qaeda types who were smuggling plastic explosives into the United States from Canada. Homeland

Security never found out what they were planning to destroy, but a bomb did blow up in Puget Sound, killing two terrorists and Chance's father.

The editor of the *Lincoln Light* that year was Melissa Watts, the daughter of a super-rich lawyer. Melissa also happened to be the semi-girlfriend of Chance Taylor. Not exactly a predictable couple: she ended up at some college like Yale, and Chance ended up in a Humvee in Iraq. But then, I'm no expert on why people hook up. Anyway, for months Melissa had suspected that Chance was involved in smuggling.

Imagine it: the editor of a high school newspaper, sitting on one of the biggest stories of the year. The hairs on the back of my neck stand up whenever I think about it. So, what does Melissa do? Does she

A) write up what she knows, send it to the *New York Times,* and transform herself into a famous journalist;

B) turn her boyfriend over to the FBI and become an instant talk-show celebrity, an American patriot with a broken heart, appearing Monday on *Oprah*; or

C) twiddle her thumbs?

If you guessed *C,* you win the washer/dryer and one year's supply of Tide.

So why didn't I step up when she backed off? A good question, and I've got a good answer. I was in middle school when this juicy stuff was going down. If an opportunity like that came my way now, I wouldn't let it slip away. Unfortunately, sleepy Seattle has gone back to being sleepy Seattle.

Still, I need a portfolio to send off to Columbia University as part of my application, so if someone steals Florence O'Day's 44EEE bra from the girls' locker room during fourth period, I'll be there, notepad open and pencil sharpened, asking questions.

3

THIS STARTED LAST SPRING, just over a year ago. I was certain I'd be elected editor of the *Lincoln Light*. I was heading into my senior year, and the editor is always a senior. I'd been on the newspaper staff longer and had written more articles than anyone else. Who else but me?

My only competition came from Alyssa Hanson, which was really no competition at all. Alyssa was shaky on the difference between *they're, their,* and *there,* and the duller her story, the more exclamation points she used.

The election took place at the May staff meeting. Mr. Dewey, the journalism teacher, passed around slips of paper, and kids scribbled their choice. He brought the slips to his desk and made tally marks on scratch paper. After a few minutes he scratched his bald head, straightened his bowtie, and stood up. "Well, Alyssa, you'll be our editor next year. Congratulations."

Alyssa beamed; everybody around her clapped, and I clapped too, a shocked smile fixed on my face. Antonio Nelson hugged her, and then Philip Yee hugged her, and then Sarah Haver hugged her, and suddenly it made sense. Alyssa Hanson had won because girls wanted to look like her and guys wanted to hug her.

Mr. Dewey put a chocolate cake and a twelve-pack of Dr. Pepper on a table in the back of the room, and we had our end-of-the-year party. As I ate a second piece of cake, I told myself that being editor wasn't a big deal. As long as I remained lead reporter, I could write stories about military recruiting on campus, drug use, gangs. If anything really exciting happened—say, one of the teachers got caught visiting X-rated Internet sites—the story would be mine.

When the party wound down, I ambled over to Alyssa. "Congratulations," I said, "and no hard feelings. I wanted to be editor, but it's not like I hate being lead reporter, so . . ." My voice trailed off.

Alyssa smiled, but it wasn't a smile I liked. "There will

be changes in assignments, Mitch. I'll be bringing my own ideas to the table, you know."

"Changes?" I said, grinning stupidly. "Like what?"

"We'll talk later, okay? Right now I want to celebrate."

I swallowed. "Well, you're the editor, Alyssa."

"That's right, Mitch. I'm the editor."

4

THAT NIGHT I COULDN'T SLEEP. Was Alyssa really going to change my assignment? And if I wasn't lead reporter, what job would she give me?

I tossed and turned, got up and ate a peanut butter sandwich, returned to bed, tossed and turned some more, had a dish of ice cream, went back to bed, and finally dozed off for a few hours. First thing the next morning, I called her.

"What do you want, Mitch? It's not even seven."

"Alyssa, if I'm not going to be lead reporter, what am I going to be?"

A long pause. "You've got to promise you won't get mad."

"I won't get mad," I said, feeling my blood start to boil. "Just tell me."

"Sports."

"Sports?"

"Mitch, you're the best writer on the staff."

"So why are you sticking me with sports?"

"Because sports is the only thing anybody actually reads. The rest of the stuff is just news, and nobody cares about the news."

"I care about the news."

"Yeah, well, you and about twenty other kids in the school."

"Why are you so sure I know about sports?"

"All guys know sports."

I didn't answer. A few seconds ticked by. "Mitch, my dad gets mad when I go over my minutes, so—"

"Who gets to be lead reporter?"

"Danni Shea," Alyssa answered.

Danni Shea? Danni Shea thought the twice-yearly sale at Nordstrom was news. "You're making Danni Shea lead writer and sticking me with sports, and you think I'm going to take it?"

"Well, yeah, I do, actually."

"Well, think again," I said, sounding like my dad. I would have slammed the phone down, only I was on my cell, so the only thing I could do was snap it shut really hard, which isn't nearly as satisfying.

5

I MADE MYSELF BREAKFAST. I didn't hear the toast pop up, so the butter didn't melt right. After I ate the toast, and two more slices with properly melted butter, I sat at the kitchen table staring at the crumbs on my plate.

Like every other male in America, I'd grown up certain that one day I'd play in the NFL or the NBA or make the majors in baseball. I was always shorter and pudgier than other kids, but I have good hand-eye coordination, so I held my own in gym class all through elementary school. Those years, I was sure that I'd grow to six four and that my flabby body would morph into pure muscle. As I watched games on TV, I'd imagine myself hitting game-winning home runs, catching last-second touchdown passes, sinking three-pointers at the buzzer.

I stopped believing I was going to be a pro in middle school, but I didn't stop watching the Seahawks and the Mariners on TV. My dad would sprawl out on the sofa, and I'd sit in the rocking chair. What's weird is that we rarely talked during the games, but we'd both remember key plays and discuss them months or even years later.

I don't just dream about being a journalist; I practice being a journalist every chance I get. I've got three marble notebooks filled with newspaper articles I've written based on movies and books. I pretend that what I've seen on the screen or read in the book actually happened. Then I get the *who, what, where, why,* and *how* down on the page just like a real reporter would.

Since middle school, I've done the same thing with all the games I watch with my dad. As the images flicker in front of me on the TV, in my head I'll compose a story:

It was fourth down and forever, with everything on the line. The quarterback dropped back to pass as his receivers streaked downfield. With the pocket collapsing around him, he stepped up and fired a long pass toward the end zone. The ball spiraled through the chill night air for what seemed an eternity, and then . . .

Give me a laptop and twenty minutes, and I can make the dullest game exciting.

So Alyssa was right—I could write sports for the *Lincoln Light.* But there was a problem. At Lincoln, *sports* meant Horst Diamond, and I was not going to spend my senior year singing the praises of Horst Diamond. It was impossible. Anybody else, okay. But not Horst.

I had to quit the *Lincoln Light.*

Newspaper is an after-school club at Lincoln High, so there's never anybody in the newspaper room during the day. During lunch I sneaked in, intending to clean out my desk. I shoved Post-its, pencils, memo pads—everything—into my backpack. It had taken three years to fill the drawer, but it took only thirty seconds to empty it.

At the bottom of the drawer sat my scrapbook. In my freshman year, I'd hole-punched fifty pages of high-quality vellum paper and carefully bound the pages together with twine. My goal had been to fill every page.

Instead of shoving the scrapbook into my backpack, I sat down and started flipping through it. There was my first article: seventy-five words on the new microphone system in the library—the first seventy-five words I'd ever had published. I kept flipping. The animal rights protest . . . the vandalism in the greenhouse . . . the changes in graduation requirements. Okay, none of the articles was earth-shattering, but I'd sweated over every word, making each story as good as it could possibly be.

The last twenty pages of my scrapbook were blank—they were for my senior year. I leafed through them anyway. The blank pages stared up at me.

I dumped all of the stuff from my pack back into the drawer, shoved the drawer closed, and left. Writing was in my blood—even if it meant writing about Horst Diamond.

I couldn't quit.

6

ONCE, HORST DIAMOND AND I had been both neighbors and best friends. I was Danny back then, and we were in elementary school. Every day after school and every day in the summer, we played together at the park by Whittier Elementary.

The park has an ancient swing set with chains that seem fifty feet long. You can swing high and far and fast— if you have the guts. My butt was permanently glued to the seat, but Horst would stand up and swing with such fury that I was afraid he'd go over the top. When he reached the highest point, he'd jump. I'd see him fly out over the wood chips, his legs churning as if he were riding a bicycle, a big smile on his big face, his blond hair streaming behind him.

I'd grip my chains tighter. He was going to die, or at least break both legs. But he'd land on his feet, hop forward, and then do it again.

Horst would fly across rings, swing like an ape through the jungle gym, climb a rope ladder to the ship's prow. I was always ten steps behind him or ten feet below him. For years, he didn't notice what a coward I was. But then came the end of our friendship: football.

The weird thing is, at first football made us tighter. In fourth and fifth grade, he had the strong arm of a QB and I had the soft hands of a wide receiver. We'd head off to the park, and pretty soon other guys would show up and we'd play touch football. Back then, I was pudgy, not fat, so I could run a down-and-out pattern and get separation from the kid guarding me, and Horst could fit the ball into the tiniest openings. Other kids were faster, but they dropped passes, and I didn't. I pictured things remaining the same throughout junior high and high school. Horst Diamond to Danny True, just like Tom Brady to Randy Moss.

In sixth grade, Horst's dad decided it was time for Horst to try out for Junior Football, so that meant I had to try out, too. I was okay with it. I pictured myself hauling in passes and running untouched into the end zone. My teammates would chest-bump me, while in the stands my mom and dad would be delirious with joy. When I pulled on my helmet and looked at myself in the mirror, the guy staring back at me was *tough*.

The day of tryouts, Coach Shoeman asked me my position.

"Wide receiver."

He looked at my gut. "You're built more like a lineman."

"Wide receiver," I insisted.

"All right, we'll try you at wide receiver."

I joined up with the four tall, skinny kids who also wanted to play wide receiver. Physically I didn't fit, but the early practices went okay because I could catch better than anybody.

Then came a full-contact scrimmage. The first play called for me was a simple slant over the middle. I went out a couple of steps and cut across the middle, just as in drills. Horst led me perfectly, just as in drills. I brought the ball in, took about half a step, and . . . *BOOM!* The ball flew in the air and I went down as if I'd been shot. That was nothing like drills. I stayed down, my head spinning. The linebacker who'd belted me was beaming. Far, far away I heard Coach Shoeman call out: "Now, that's a hit, men. That's what we're after."

I wobbled off the field to the bench. After what seemed like a long time, Shoeman came over. "Next time, brace yourself after you make the catch. You've got to hang on to the ball."

I nodded.

"Okay. Get back out there, and remember what I told you."

The first two plays were runs, but on third down and three, Horst called the slant pass again. "Don't drop it this time," he barked. "We need this first down."

On the snap, I took two steps forward and made my cut. I tried to concentrate on the ball, but my eyes searched instead for the linebacker who'd laid me out before. Horst's pass hit me in the chest, right between the numbers, and bounced away. A millisecond later, the same guy unloaded on me again.

For the second time I climbed off the deck and wobbled to the sideline. Five minutes . . . ten minutes . . . fifteen minutes. I sat on the bench, head woozy and legs like rubber. When the scrimmage was just about over, Shoeman came back to me. "Next punt, I want you out there on the coverage team."

I watched the game, praying there wouldn't be another punt, but there was. Shoeman nodded to me and clapped his hands. "You've been hit hard twice. Now *you* hit someone." I pulled on my helmet and lined up as a wide-out. The punter booted the ball, and I raced downfield, praying somebody else would tackle the returner, and quickly.

At first the play was moving away from me, but the punt returner suddenly reversed field, broke into the clear, and now was barreling right at me. I was the last guy with a shot to tackle him. When he was right in front of me, I lurched to the side as if he were a bull and I were a matador, and he roared by me. I spun around and watched him cross the goal line. When I turned back, Horst was glaring at me.

Shoeman blew his whistle. "Same time tomorrow."

I was dragging myself off the field when Shoeman called me back. He looked down at me as if I were a stink-bug. "A football player has to be able to take a hit. If you can't, you need to quit this game and find another."

I didn't find another game, but I did quit, and Horst stopped knocking on my door.

That summer, Lenny Westwood's family moved into the brick house on the corner. Westwood is a tall, skinny black kid with a quick first step and good hands, exactly the friend Horst wanted. In the fall Horst's mom had her twin girls, and by December they'd moved into their huge house near Sunset Hill Park.

7

AT THE NEXT NEWSPAPER MEETING, Alyssa did a double take when she saw me at the big table in the center of the room, and then she came over. "I thought you were quitting," she said quietly.

"I never said that."

"I thought you did."

"Well, I didn't."

"I'm glad, because you can add a lot to the newspaper."

"Thank you, Alyssa," I said. "That's nice of you to say."

"It's true, Mitch. I mean Dan."

"Call me Mitch."

Her long brown hair had fallen into her face, so she pushed it behind her ear. "This'll work, Mitch. And who knows? You might uncover a big sports story that will shake all of Seattle."

"Sure," I said. "And maybe I'll star in a Hollywood movie."

Her temper flashed. "Well, you don't know for sure, do you? It could happen."

"What? Me starring in a movie?"

"Very funny." She rose, but before she walked away, she fixed me with a steely stare. "Mitch, if you're not going to do the job right, tell me and I'll get somebody else."

"Don't worry. I'll do my job."

She stayed on me. "That means you'll have a football preview ready to go for September's issue. And you'll cover girls' volleyball, too."

She was being serious, so I owed her a serious answer. "I won't have time for any minor sports. But I will do the major sports, both girls and boys, all year long, and that's a promise."

She nodded. "I'm going to surprise you, Mitch. Last year there were four newspapers. I'm going to put one out every month, or close to it. And every single one of them is going to be better than anything we did last year. That's a promise, too."

She walked to the front of the room and called everyone to attention. As she ran the meeting, I thought about big sports stories that reporters had broken. There'd been articles on steroids, and there'd been a book on Bobby Knight and how crazy he was as a coach. The more I thought, the more I came up with. Baseball, basketball, football, cycling, soccer—every sport had stories that went way beyond the games. I'd have to get lucky, but maybe Alyssa would be right. Maybe something would happen at Lincoln.

8

THE FIRST FOOTBALL PRACTICE was August 15. Lincoln's coach, Hal McNulty, is one of those gruff, Marine-sergeant types: crew-cut hair, bulging muscles, pants and shirt pressed, shoes shined. He's a PE teacher as well as a coach, and I had him my sophomore year. Some PE teachers ignore fat guys, and some torture them. He was a torturer. He made me attempt every gymnastic move, including cartwheels, and he snickered when I flopped on the mat like a tortoise without a shell.

He'd had a head coaching job at some Division II college in the Midwest but had gotten himself fired for having tutors write essays for the players who didn't know their left shoe from their right ear, or at least that was the rumor. When he was first hired at Lincoln, he told Chet Jetton, the high school sports reporter for the *Seattle Times,* that his goal was to win a state title so he could get back into college coaching.

I don't know whether it is because of McNulty's coaching or Horst's quarterbacking, but Lincoln has taken the league the past two years, though both times they lost in the first round of the playoffs. Those losses had to eat at McNulty—he'd come so close.

I work afternoons in the summer at my parents' business, so it was early in the morning on August 14 when I headed to Lincoln High hoping to corner McNulty before practices started and get him to talk. I wanted him to respect me as a reporter, so before I left, I stood in front of the mirror and practiced sucking in my gut as I introduced myself. *"Hello, Coach, I'm Mitch True. I'll be covering the team for the* Lincoln Light *this year."* I tried three or four different voices, but none sounded right. Besides, regardless of the voice I used, I had to breathe, and when I did, my flabby gut would hang over my belt.

I parked my mom's Ford Focus by the gym, eased out of the front seat, and looked around. When I spotted McNulty loading tackling sleds into a school van, I tensed. To him, I'd always be a fat loser and nothing more. But a reporter has to have the courage to approach people, ask them questions, and get them to talk. "I'm Mitch True," I said as I neared him. "I'm the school sports reporter. I'd like to ask you some questions."

"I was hoping you'd come around," he said. "Step into my office."

I gaped, dumbfounded. *He was hoping I'd come around?* When I recovered, I nearly had to run to catch up as he strode across the field and into the coaches' office in the gym. He took a seat behind a neatly organized desk while I squeezed into a wobbly blue plastic chair across from him.

"What's your name again?"

I told him again.

"You were in my gym class last year, right?"

"Two years ago."

"Well, Mr. True, you are now an important member of the Lincoln Mustangs football family."

I smiled.

"What's funny?" McNulty said, his blue-gray eyes glittering like shiny stones.

Like an idiot, I patted my jiggly belly. "Me? An important member of the football family? How?"

He leaned forward, pointing his pencil at me. "You are the person who sends in a game recap to the *Seattle Times*. You write exciting articles, and the *Times* will push them to the top of the high school page. That happens, and other newspapers will pick them up, which translates into publicity for the players and for me. It also means a byline for you, some cash, and a summer internship to boot. You remember last year's sports writer, Boyd Harte. He interned at the *Bellevue Journal*."

I hadn't thought about the connections I'd be making, but as sports stringer, I'd be dealing with editors of real newspapers, something that wouldn't have happened if I'd remained the news reporter for the *Lincoln Light*—unless the big dailies suddenly became interested in the accomplishments of Lincoln High's chess club. "Sounds great," I said. "In fact, it sounds fantastic."

McNulty leaned back. "See. We're all part of one big family."

I cleared my throat. "How about we get started? I've got some questions. First—"

"No, no, no," McNulty said, pointing the pencil at me again. "No questions—not today, not ever. This job takes forever and pays peanuts. Here's how it works. You write down or tape what I tell you. When I'm done, jazz it up however you want, but never make me, my coaches, or my players look bad. Understand?"

Mr. Dewey had warned us about people like McNulty, but this was my first time dealing with one. "A reporter who lets himself be pushed around is a traitor to his profession." That's what Dewey had said.

I could feel myself trying to say: *"Coach, I will ask the questions I want to ask, and I will write what I want to write."*

In the classroom, practicing with bald, bowtied Mr. Dewey, I had spit out similar words like a machine gun spits out bullets. But McNulty's eyes were scary. I squirmed as he stared at me, feeling like a snot-nosed preschooler who'd been caught marking a wall with crayons. "Understood?" he said again, a threat in his voice, as though he might force me to do cartwheels in front of the football team if I argued.

"Yes, sir."

From a drawer he took out three sheets of paper covered with black type and shoved them at me. "Here's the information for the football preview. Horst Diamond will be the focus, and you'll be leading every game story with his name, too. He's a lock for a D-I scholarship. UW is drooling over him, but he's got a shot at a bigger school—Notre Dame, or even USC. Your job is to get him publicity."

I scanned the three sheets. "But what if somebody else has a better game?"

"Nobody's going to have a better game. Run or pass—everything we do goes through Horst. I want a swarm of college coaches around here. They'll see him, and they'll see me and the program I run. I do not intend to spend my life coaching high school."

McNulty stood. "Read those pages, prepare a few questions, and before practice tomorrow you can interview Horst. He'll be at the field fifteen minutes early. Have your photographer come along for that." He paused. "You've got a photographer, right?"

"A photographer?"

"Every sports story needs pictures. Either you've got to take them yourself, or you've got to get a photographer. Didn't you know that?"

9

BACK HOME, I washed down an almond pastry with a cup of hot chocolate. While I ate, my mind spun in circles. When Mr. Dewey had told us to be courageous, he'd been talking about journalists uncovering corruption. But Coach McNulty? Horst Diamond? They were just sports figures. Sports is—well—sports. So why make a big deal out of nothing?

As I started on a second almond pastry, I remembered what McNulty had said about the photographer. All I know about cameras is that I hate having my picture taken. I called Alyssa.

"Relax, Mitch," she said. "I've got you a photographer."

"You do? Who?"

"Kimi Yon."

"Kimi Yon?"

"She's into sports photography, or at least that's what she says. Personally, I think she wants to get some photos published because that would look good on her college applications. Harvard, Yale, and Princeton are the only schools good enough for her."

"You don't like Kimi?"

"I like her okay. I'm just being bitchy. Don't tell her what I said, okay?"

"I won't." I paused. "Does Kimi know she'll be working with me?"

"Mitch, don't say it that way. Besides, it's not like she's going to the Winter Ball with you." Alyssa laughed at the thought, and I managed to laugh along.

"Could you give me her number? I've got an interview tomorrow with Horst Diamond."

"It's 789-9365. Mitch, I'm sorry. What I said was mean."

"Forget it."

"Look, I've got to get off. I told you about my dad and minutes. "

Kids who don't like Kimi joke that there are actually two Kimis: the one who gets an A on everything and the one who gets an A+. When I first met her, I thought she was totally into herself and her grades, but my opinion of her changed one day in AP American History.

We were the only sophomores in a class filled with juniors and seniors. Our teacher, Ms. Simonson, was new. "I'm going to use the same methods that Socrates used in ancient Greece." That's what she said on the first day, her eyes shining, and every day she tried to get discussions going. Most days, nothing much happened. She wasn't a great teacher, but she worked harder than any teacher I've ever had.

Ms. Simonson was also short, fat, and ugly. Early in November the seniors started calling her Yoda, after the little Zen guy from Star Wars. They'd whisper, but they'd whisper so loudly that everyone could hear. I laughed the first time; she did look a lot like Yoda.

Only they wouldn't stop. Mario Chalmers, a basketball player and one of the big shots in the school, was the worst. He'd make some Yoda comment, and his friends would roll around in their chairs and laugh. Ms. Simonson pretended not to hear, but her face would turn bright red. It was like watching somebody pull the wings off a fly. What could I do, though? I was Mitch, and he was Mario Chalmers.

Then, one Friday, Kimi Yon stood up, right in the middle of class, and glared at Chalmers. "Stop it!" she shouted after he'd made yet another Yoda joke. "Just stop it!" Her eyes glowed with rage. "You're not funny."

The whole room fell silent. Even Ms. Simonson stood like a statue. Chalmers's face looked as if a vampire had sucked the blood out of him. He glanced around for help, but his buddies had their heads down. He turned back to Kimi, and her eyes were still on fire. He shrugged, dropped his head onto his chest, and slouched deep into his chair. After that, Chalmers and his friends messed around some, but they never called Ms. Simonson Yoda again.

Now Alyssa had just told me that Kimi Yon—beautiful, brilliant, courageous Kimi Yon—was going to be my partner. If I had been any other guy, I'd have been out-of-my-mind happy at the thought. But I wasn't any other guy, and that was the problem.

Even though I make jokes about being fat, that doesn't mean I'm happy about it. When school ended in mid-June, I promised myself that I wouldn't return to Lincoln in September with a stomach as soft as a jelly roll. But once you get out of shape, it's hard to get back into shape. And my parents' business doesn't make it any easier.

They run a catering service that supplies fancy desserts to expensive restaurants like Ray's Boathouse and Canlis. Because they run their own business, I never have to job hunt. They don't believe in having me work during the school year, but in the summer I put in twenty hours a week, mainly helping with the afternoon deliveries.

That's the good part. The bad part is that bakeries are always bringing new pastries to my mom, and I'm her guinea pig. Every night after dinner, my dad goes off to read the newspaper, leaving my mom and me alone in the kitchen. She puts a piece of chocolate cake or peach-blueberry pie slathered in whipped cream in front of me. Then she sits down across from me, her own dessert in front of her. "Try a few bites, Dan," she says. "I want to know what you think."

Once either of us starts eating a dessert, we don't stop until it's gone, which is why we're both overweight while my dad isn't. I finish the whole thing, grade it as though I'm some sort of food expert, and my mom smiles and thanks me. It's as if eating huge desserts is part of my job. So June and July and half of August had slipped by, and pies and cakes had slipped down my throat. And now I'd be going places with Kimi Yon. Standing next to her, I'd look fatter and shorter and paler. If only I'd started exercising and stopped eating.

There was no point in postponing the inevitable. I flipped open my cell phone, punched in the numbers as fast as I could, and hit the green call button.

"Hello." A man's voice—her father. Alyssa had given me Kimi's home number, not her cell.

My palms got sweaty. "Is Kimi home?"

"Who is this? My daughter not talk to boys unless I know."

"I'm Mitch True. I'm the sports—"

In the background I heard her voice. "Dad, give me the phone." Her father said something in what I figured was Chinese, and then Kimi came on the line. "Hello. Who is this?"

"It's Mitch True," I said. "You know me, I think, from Ms. Simonson's class. But maybe you don't know me. I'm sort of—" I stopped. How could I describe myself?

"I know you, Mitch. Everybody knows you. I'm glad to be working with you."

"You are?"

"Sure. You're the best writer in the school." She paused. "When do we start?"

I swallowed. "Well, I've got an interview with Horst Diamond scheduled for tomorrow, and pictures would be great."

"Okay. What time?"

"Eight forty-five at Gilman Park."

"The Fifteen bus goes right by Gilman. I'll be there."

In the summer my mom always drove in to work with my dad so that I could use her car. I took a deep breath. "I can give you a ride."

Silence.

I'd crossed the line—Kimi wouldn't want to be seen in the same car with me. "Look," I said, "it's okay if you'd rather take the bus."

"I'd rather get a ride. It's just that my father is so weird. He's the most incredibly stereotypical Asian dad. He'll ask you a million questions, and then he'll follow you down the street shouting driving instructions."

"I don't care," I said, thinking that he couldn't be that bad.

She sighed. "All right. My address is—"

I wrote down the number. "See you at eight twenty," I said.

I closed my cell, amazed. Kimi *wanted* to work with me.

Before heading to work that afternoon, I drove to Brown Bear car wash. I washed the car, wiped it dry, and vacuumed the seats and the floor. When I finished it looked better, but it was still a ten-year-old silver Ford Focus with a dented front passenger fender and a missing rear wheel cover.

I woke early Tuesday morning and showered. I toweled dry, dug out my bottle of Calvin Klein Obsession, and sprayed a little on. But then I felt ridiculous—we weren't going on a date—and washed it off. For breakfast I ate a vanilla yogurt and half a cinnamon bagel—no butter. Starting *now* I was getting in shape.

Five minutes later I pulled up in front of Kimi's house on Cleopatra Place. I'd driven by it before, not because I was stalking her (I'm fat and ugly, not a pervert), but because Cleopatra is a good shortcut when Eighth Avenue backs up, and I'd seen her in front of her house.

My dad fights weeds all the time, and our yard looks good, but Kimi's yard made my dad's garden look like Kit

Carson's wilderness. It was as if Mr. Yon's flowers were on steroids, while weeds knew better than to poke their ugly heads out of the ground.

I strode up the walkway to the front door, but it swung open before I reached it. "Come in," her father said, "but no shoes." He was smiling and bowing, but his eyes were fierce. I looked around for Kimi's mother, and then I remembered hearing that Kimi's mother was dead.

I kicked off my shoes. Kimi was perched on a snow-white sofa, her head bowed and the palms of her hands pressing against her forehead. She wore faded jeans and a U2 T-shirt. Her sunglasses were pushed up into her hair. "We've got to go, Dad."

"You sit down," Mr. Yon said, ignoring her.

I sat. "I'm Mitch True."

"You wear seat belt?"

"Yes. Always."

"Dad."

"And you drive slow."

"Yes, sir. I drive slow."

"You make sure Kimi wear seat belt, and you drive slow."

"Yes, Mr. Yon. I will."

"Dad, we've got to go," Kimi said, moving toward the door. I followed, yanking my shoes back on. She almost ran down the walkway; she was in the passenger seat before I was halfway to the car.

"Oh my God, he is *so* embarrassing," Kimi said as we pulled away. "He acts like I'm going be kidnapped and forced to become a sex slave in Thailand."

I pictured Mr. Yon sitting alone in his spotless house, worried sick. Who could blame him? Kimi was amazing, and he'd just seen me—me!—drive off with her.

"He just cares a lot," I said, sounding like my mom.

10

ONCE I'D PULLED INTO an empty parking space at Gilman Park and killed the engine, I turned to Kimi. "We'll do the interview first. Then you can take photos of Horst."

Kimi pursed her lips. "For three years it's been nothing but Horst. Everybody at Lincoln is sick of him, except for Britt Lind, and I bet she's sick of him too. Let's look for somebody new."

I cleared my throat. How could I tell Kimi that Coach McNulty was calling the shots? She'd have stood up to him the same way she'd stood up to Mario Chalmers.

"Sure," I said, "if there is somebody new. But if Horst is the best player—"

"You're right. Still, we can keep our eyes open."

We walked across the field toward the west corner

where McNulty waited, clipboard in hand. Horst loomed next to him, gripping and regripping a leather football. McNulty looked at his watch as we neared. "Practice starts in seventeen minutes. Once it begins, the interview ends." And then he was gone.

Horst was wearing shorts and a muscle shirt. He must have spent the summer at the beach and in the gym because his bulging biceps were deep bronze. He smiled, his teeth bleached weirdly white. "Hey, Kimi, you here to interview me?"

Kimi nodded toward me. "Mitch does the interview; I take the photos."

Horst's eyes never left Kimi. "I look best holding the ball up like this, like I'm scanning the field for a receiver." He flexed. Was there a new movie, *Son of Popeye,* that I hadn't heard about? Did he think he was auditioning for the lead?

"I like candid shots," Kimi said. "Real life, not faked."

He pulled the ball down. "You're the photographer." He turned to me. "Fire away."

The night before, I'd come up with oddball questions that would make him squirm. My best was *If you were a girl, what guy on the team would you want to date?*

I'd had fun dreaming up those questions, but with two hundred pounds of Horst muscle standing in front of me, I fell back on the regular stuff. What goals had he set for himself? For the team? What areas did he need to improve?

The answers were the usual yawners. He needed to improve every part of his game. Personal goals would take care of themselves if the team did well. Blah, blah, blah.

While Horst blathered on, Kimi wandered off. As soon as she was out of earshot, Horst nudged me. "She looks fit, doesn't she? I'd like to be part of her workout routine, if you get my meaning." He laughed, but when I didn't join in, he stopped.

I asked a few more standard questions, and then sucked up my courage for one of my out-of-the-box questions. "What scares you, Horst? What really, really scares you?"

His face went blank, and then he shrugged. "That's a dumb question. Why would anything scare me?"

I looked at him. Athletic, handsome, popular, and rich. He was right: it had been a dumb question. "All right," I said. "That does it."

As I closed my notebook, a strange thing happened. Horst reached out, rested his hand on my shoulder, and looked me in the eye. "Mitch, I want you to know, you need an interview or a quote, you call me, day or night. I'm never too busy for the press. You understand? I mean— we're friends, right?"

"Sure we're friends."

Then he squeezed my shoulder before jogging off to join his teammates.

I hated myself. I mean—how weak was that? For years the guy blows me off, and then—when he needs me to get his name in the newspaper—he gives me a phony smile, and I lick his fingers like a homeless puppy.

Kimi had gone across the field over to the children's play area. She'd taken off her shoes and was sitting on the edge of the wading pool, dangling her toes in the water. I trudged over, and she turned to me, her mouth drawn tight. "I don't know how you can stand talking to him. Just because he's got a great body, he thinks the whole world will swoon over him. We can't feature Horst, Mitch. I don't think I can get my camera to focus on him."

I felt beads of sweat forming under my arms. "But, if he's the best—"

"Who's that?" she said, her finger pointing toward a guy wearing a Philadelphia Eagles jersey. He was playing catch with some man in a Seahawks sweatshirt—an older brother or friend, probably—way off in a corner of the practice field.

"I don't know."

"He wasn't here last year; I'd have noticed him. He's pretty good, isn't he?"

I've watched enough games to recognize a player with a great arm, and the kid Kimi pointed out was zinging the ball like an NFL quarterback. His passes had so much zip, I half expected to see jets of flame behind them. He had the size of an NFL quarterback, too. I'd guess six three and 220.

I looked over to the main practice field. Horst was passing the ball to his old buddy Lenny Westwood. I watched Horst throw, and then turned back to the kid wearing the Eagles jersey. The new guy looked bigger and stronger. With that arm, he'd bring a deep threat to the offense. A tingle ran up and down my spine. Could Horst lose his starting job?

A shrill blast on a whistle was followed by McNulty's voice through a bullhorn. "Everyone over here." The new guy threw one more frozen rope before trotting toward McNulty. Kimi turned back to me. "Let's interview him later. I bet he's got a story."

WE CLIMBED TO THE TOP of a little hill to watch practice. The players were in shorts with no helmets. McNulty had them running forward, backwards, sideways left, sideways right. Then they'd do push-ups, sit-ups, jumping jacks, stretches, run through tires, run through ropes, hit tackling sleds. "Well," Kimi said after a while. "What do you think?"

"About what?"

"About interviewing the guy wearing the number five jersey."

"It's a good idea, Kimi, but we can't just go talk to him."

"Why not?"

"Because we've got to check with McNulty first."

"Why?"

"Coaches control access to their players."

She held the camera up to her face, and then handed it to me. "Mitch, look at his eyes."

I focused the camera and then used the zoom to pull in close.

"Do you see it?" she said.

"See what?"

"The haunted look. His eyes are old and sad. He's lived through more than anybody else out there."

I peered through the camera. I tried to see a *haunted look,* but I don't know what *haunted* looks like. He did look old, though. I'd have guessed he was twenty-two or twenty-three if I hadn't known he was in high school. I handed back the camera. "Sometime I'll ask McNulty if we can interview him," I said.

"Ask him now, Mitch."

"I can't interrupt practice," I protested.

As if on cue, McNulty blew his whistle. "Water break. Ten minutes." Then he climbed down from his makeshift coaching tower and walked toward his assistant coaches.

"Come on," Kimi said, and before I could answer, she broke into a jog to intercept him. But a jog for her is a sprint for me. For the millionth time, I told myself that I had to lose weight.

"Coach," she yelled when we got within ten feet of McNulty.

He stopped and turned around. "What?"

I was panting so hard I couldn't speak. Kimi saw me gasping. "Mitch wants to interview the guy wearing the number five jersey."

McNulty looked at me. "Why?"

I'd caught my breath a little. "He was throwing off to the side," I panted. "And he's got an NFL arm. He throws harder than Horst."

McNulty stared at me as if I were from outer space. "Harder than Horst? Like an NFL quarterback?"

I felt like a foolish five-year-old, but I plunged on. "Have him throw for you. You'll see."

McNulty looked up at the sky, disgust on his face. "One hour and the kid knows more than I do about my own team."

I didn't back down. "Just—"

"You, the guy wearing the Philly jersey," McNulty's voice boomed out, interrupting me. "Come over here. Coby Eliot, you come too."

The two players trotted over to where we were standing. McNulty looked toward Kimi and me. My face and neck flashed hot and red, which always happens when I get excited.

"What's your name, son?" McNulty asked Number Five.

"Angel Marichal," came the whispered answer. Up close, he seemed even bigger.

"Where you from, Angel?"

"Houston."

"You play football last year?"

"I got cut. It was a big school."

McNulty shot me a look, then turned back to Marichal.

"What's your position, Marichal?"

"Linebacker."

"Ever play quarterback?"

He shook his head. "No, sir."

McNulty nodded toward me. "This guy thinks you throw the ball like a professional quarterback."

Angel shook his head. "I'm not a quarterback," he repeated.

"Throw a few for me anyway," McNulty said.

Angel shrugged, and then stepped off to the side to play catch with Coby Eliot. I looked at Kimi, and her dark eyes glittered with excitement. Maybe Angel didn't know how good he was, but we did. Soon McNulty would know, too.

Coby Eliot stood about twenty-five yards from Angel Marichal. Angel cocked his arm, and I waited for the ball to sizzle through the summer air, waited for McNulty's eyebrows to go up, waited for him to look at Kimi and me with respect.

Only the ball didn't sizzle. It looped, high in the air. It wobbled off to the right. Eliot ran under it, caught it, and flung it back. Again Marichal threw. Again a pathetic moon-ball drifted in the general direction of Eliot. A third pass, a fourth, a fifth. All moon shots.

"That's enough," McNulty said. "Go on, get back with the other guys."

Eliot and Marichal trotted off; McNulty wheeled on me. "Like an NFL pro?"

"He threw a hundred times better before," I mumbled, feeling ridiculous. "A thousand times."

McNulty scowled. "The next time you discover the second coming of Joe Montana, call ESPN. Don't bother me again. Understand?"

"We still want to interview him," Kimi insisted. "He's a fresh face."

"Well, you're not interviewing him," McNulty barked.

"Why not?" Kimi persisted.

"Because I've got twenty-two seniors on this team who've busted their butts for Lincoln for three years. Angel, or whatever the hell his name is, hasn't finished his first practice. You write about those guys and then talk to me about a new guy." With that, McNulty spun around and headed back to his assistants.

I turned to Kimi. "You want to go?"

"I haven't taken pictures of Horst yet," she said, her voice trembling.

We returned to our spot on the grassy hill and sat looking down at the practice field as McNulty and his assistants ran the players through more drills. Kimi trained her camera on Horst and snapped photo after photo, but I kept my eyes glued on Angel Marichal.

In every drill, Angel was mediocre, which made no sense. There was no way Kimi and I had imagined those bullet passes or the natural athleticism. I leaned back on my elbows and chewed on a blade of grass.

Something was missing. Mr. Dewey always told us to look for just this situation. He said that a reporter's job is to find that missing piece. This wasn't a big, earth-shaking, terrorist story like Melissa Watts had had her hands on. But it was a story.

"What's wrong?" Kimi said, pulling the camera away from her face.

I nodded toward the field. "Angel. He's not really trying."

McNulty had the players doing shuttle runs, checking their quickness. Angel was constantly adjusting his speed, making sure he stayed near the middle of the pack. Kimi watched, and then turned to me. "You're right. And he's not very good at faking." She paused. "Why would you try out for a team and then not try?"

"I don't know, but he's got a story. And before the season is over, we're going to get it."

As soon as I finished my little speech, I felt dumb. Who did I think I was—some big-time CNN reporter? I peeked at Kimi. I was afraid she'd be laughing at me, but she wasn't, and I liked her even more.

12

KIMI TOOK PHOTOS for another ten minutes, and then put the lens cap on her camera. "You have time to go to Peet's?" Peet's is a coffee shop in Fremont, the trendiest neighborhood in Seattle. I gaped, speechless. She wanted to go to Peet's with me? "Or do you have stuff to do?"

"I work, but not until the afternoon. Peet's sounds great."

Ten minutes later Kimi was ordering Chai tea. I wanted a large mocha with whipped cream, but I ordered tea. I nodded toward the chocolate biscotti in the glass jar on the counter. "You want one?"

She shook her head. "I just ate breakfast."

Just ate breakfast! I thought. *That was two hours ago.*

What I said was "I'm not hungry either."

From an upstairs counter, we looked out the window and watched people strolling along Fremont Avenue, some stopping to browse in the music shop or one of the vintage clothes shops. Most were in their twenties, and none seemed as if they were headed to work or school. Seeing them drifting about in the late morning would have driven my dad crazy. Delivery drivers were always quitting on him. I could almost hear him: *"Young people just don't know the meaning of work."*

Kimi stirred one packet of sugar into her tea. "I want to help out with the Angel story. You'll need photos, won't you?"

"Yeah. If there really is a story."

She sipped her tea. "He's got a story. I can see it in his eyes. He's gone through something." She put her cup down. "Where do we begin?"

"The way to do this," I said, feeling my way as I spoke, "is to brainstorm. Get all our ideas out and then sort the good from the bad."

She nodded. "Okay. Let's start with what we know. First, we know Angel is new to Seattle. Second, we know he's from Houston. And third, we know he got cut from his school's football team last year."

"I don't buy the last one. I don't care how big his high school was. With his size, he'd make the team."

Kimi considered. "Maybe he made the team but got kicked off for drugs or alcohol. Maybe he's pretending to be mediocre so McNulty won't check on his past."

"That's possible, but there's another possibility, too."

"What?"

"He could be cheating."

"Cheating? How?"

"You heard about that kid in the Little League World Series?"

"No. Tell me."

"Danny something. It happened years ago. He claimed he was twelve but he was really sixteen. He was a pitcher, and he struck out everybody. When he got caught, his team had to forfeit their title. Maybe Angel Marichal screwed up somewhere and now he's trying to sneak in one more year of high school football even though he's not eligible. "

"But if that's Angel's story, wouldn't he want to be a star? He wouldn't come back, play poorly at practice, and end up sitting on the bench, would he?"

"Probably not," I admitted.

We fell silent. Kimi finished her tea; I let the bottom inch of mine go cold.

"Okay, we're done brainstorming. What's next?" she asked.

"Now we start investigating. I'll Google him, then follow up whatever I get."

13

SPENDING TIME WITH KIMI, having a story to investigate—all of that was good. What wasn't good was the way I'd huffed and puffed to keep up with her as she'd chased down McNulty.

Lots of times I'd come up with a plan for getting into shape—diet or exercise or both—but after a week or so, I'd stop. I'd tell myself that I'd start up again in a month, but that *now* just wasn't the right time.

But now *was* the right time. Kimi made it the right time. We'd be covering boys' football and girls' volleyball together, and other sports later in the year. What had

Alyssa said—that I wasn't such a bad guy? I was almost certain Kimi didn't have a boyfriend, that she hung out in a group, not with one guy.

If I lost ten pounds a month, I'd be down to 170 by December. Maybe I'd even grow those couple of inches my dad has always promised me. Alyssa had been joking, but if I was five foot six and weighed 170, I might just ask Kimi to the Winter Ball. If I was five six and weighed 170, Kimi might just say yes.

I changed into a sweatshirt and sweatpants and drove to Green Lake. Mr. Johnson, my biology teacher, had said that fat people think they should lose weight and then start exercising. Johnson said that if a fat person got into shape, the weight would drop off naturally.

The last time I'd exercised was over a year ago when I'd signed up to play basketball at the community center. The league was supposed to be low-key, and I'm actually an okay basketball player. I can't rebound, but I can dribble with either hand and I can shoot lights out. Give me time to set my feet, and it's *swish!*

Most of the guys in the league didn't care about winning, but I was assigned to Larry Wolf's team, and Wolf hates to lose. "Give it your all," Wolf said to me before the first game. "We need you."

We played man-to-man defense, and I had to guard Craig Ruskin, a short kid with droopy eyes, a thick mop of hair, and sharp elbows. Ruskin scored six points early, but then seemed to stop trying. Late in the game I dropped in four long bombs of my own. We won 38–30 and Wolf was crazy with joy. "I didn't know you could shoot like that!" he said, slapping me on the back.

I felt pretty good about myself until we walked off the court and Ruskin sidled up next to me. "That's quite a secret weapon you've got," he said.

"What is?"

He nodded at my drenched shirt. "The way you sweat. All fat guys sweat, but you really sweat. Made me want to stay clear." He gave me a dumb smile. "No offense."

That ended by basketball career.

The path around Green Lake stretches nearly three miles. I've seen people running it for as long as I can remember: thin girls with long legs, hair pulled through the back of baseball caps, iPods strapped to their arms; muscular football players with powerful strides; lean soccer players with loping strides. But there were other people on the path besides athletes. Middle-aged men and women with paunchy stomachs. Dog-walkers, Rollerbladers, creaky old people, little kids on bikes.

I parked the Focus by the pitch-and-putt golf course and went to a post to stretch. Instantly I had the feeling that everyone was staring at me, thinking: *What's that fat, weirdly white guy stretching for?* But then an older man with gray hair stuck his leg on the post next to mine and nodded. I nodded back, feeling as if I belonged.

After a couple minutes, I started around the lake. I'd intended to walk, but seeing all the runners gave me the courage to jog. Everything went okay for a grand total of fifty yards. That's when I spotted Andrea Porter and Maddy Lee, both of whom were on the cross-country team. Maddy was tall and thin, with black hair and a long, silky stride. Andrea was a short blonde whose legs churned.

I panicked. If they saw me, they'd tell other kids, and then those other kids would tell other kids. *You won't believe who was running Green Lake!*

I turned off the path and headed down to the water where the men stand with their tackle boxes and their fishing poles. One grizzly-looking guy eyed me suspiciously. I tried to make conversation. "What do you catch?" I asked.

"Trout. You fish?"

"No."

"Hmm," he grunted, and turned away.

When I looked back to the path, Andrea and Maddy had passed; I could see their ponytails swinging in rhythm with their strides. I retraced my steps to the car and drove off.

14

THE *MITCH-BEFORE-KIMI* would have driven home, gone into the house, and headed straight to the refrigerator. But I was determined to get in shape. I was *not* going to be fat all my life.

Instead of going home, I drove to the Ballard Locks. I did one quick circuit around the garden—walking, not running—but when I finished I hadn't even broken a sweat.

I didn't want to go endlessly around and around the path, so I headed across the Locks and into the Magnolia neighborhood. Rachel Black and some other rich kids from Lincoln live in Magnolia, but they live on the fancy west side where the streets have names like Viewmont or Crestmont or Glenmont. I turned east into the industrial section, taking Commodore Way past the old warehouses and the junker homes.

I walked a block, then ran a block, walked, then ran. After ten minutes, my heart was thumping and my shirt was drenched in sweat. But so what? Craig Ruskin wasn't around. I ran/jogged all the way to Fishermen's Terminal, where I turned around. The return trip was uphill, so I was completely exhausted by the time I reached the Focus, but I felt good. This time I was going to stick with it.

I showered, ate an apple and a bagel—no cream cheese—and then went to work at my parents' business. They'd hired yet another new driver, so I had to give him directions to all the restaurants on our list. Still, he drove fast, so we finished by four thirty.

My parents work later than that, which is why the Focus is basically my car. I drove home, went up to my room, opened my laptop, and did a search for *Angel Marichal*. For twenty minutes I tried different links and different searches, but none led anywhere.

I closed up the laptop and went downstairs. Instead of eating, I poured a large glass of water and sipped it slowly while I flipped through a brochure I'd gotten in the mail from some small college in Kentucky. I was still at the kitchen table when my mom and dad returned. My dad disappeared into our TV room to watch the news, but my mom joined me in the kitchen. In her hand she held a clear plastic bag filled with three blueberry muffins. She laid the bag on the table in front of me.

"How was your day?"

"Maybe you could stop bringing stuff like that home," I said, nodding toward the bag.

"The muffins?"

"Muffins. Croissants. Cakes. Pies. All of it. Please, just leave it at work."

She shrugged. "Okay, but really, Dan, there's no harm in just a few bites."

"But I never have just a few bites. I eat the whole thing, and sometimes I have seconds. I've got to stop; I need to lose weight."

"Oh, you'll slim down as you get older."

"I'm seventeen," I snapped. I grabbed my belly and shook it. "This isn't baby fat. It's fat. I'm fat."

She'd been bustling about, putting things away, but now she stopped and turned to me. For a moment she didn't speak, but I could see her eyes well up with tears. "It's my fault," she said, her voice thick with emotion. "I know it is. Your father has said the same thing. But you always loved desserts. Cookies, cakes, candies—all of them made you happy, and I wanted you happy, so I gave them to you."

I was afraid she was going to start sobbing. Why had I yelled at her? And how was it her fault? I was the one who stuffed the food into my mouth. I stood and put my arm around her shoulder. "I'm not blaming you, Mom. Really, I'm not. I enjoy the food. Only now I need to change, and you can help."

She picked up the bag of muffins and moved it to the refrigerator. "Your father and I will eat these. And after this, I won't bring any desserts home." She closed the refrigerator door and left.

I needed to say what I'd said, or something like it, but I still felt bad. Both she and my dad let me be myself, which is all you can ask from parents. They pushed science at me from first grade on, but when I told them I wanted to be a newspaper reporter, they didn't try to talk me out of it. Same thing with Columbia. It's the last college in the world my mom would have picked for me. She's terrified I'll get killed by some New York City gang guy, but if Columbia takes me, she'll let me go. It was just with food that she'd messed up; everything else she did okay.

PART TWO

PART TWO

I **EXERCISED EVERY DAY** for the next ten days. I stayed with my same route through the industrial part of Magnolia, across from the Ballard Locks. I'd run two blocks, walk one on the way out; run one block and walk two on the way back.

I was weighing myself constantly, but that started making me loony. I'd drink water or wear a sweatshirt, and my weight would go up, and I'd want to scream. Finally I decided to weigh myself first thing every Monday morning. Well, second thing. First I'd pee and get rid of however much a morning pee weighs.

During that time, I didn't call Kimi. I knew she'd want to talk about my investigation, which was getting nowhere. I'd tried a couple of other search engines besides Google, but the only Angel Marichal I discovered lived in Miami, lip-synched Ricky Martin songs, and raised tortoises. Definitely not our guy. What was I supposed to do next? Tap Angel's phone? Ransack his house?

Monday morning Alyssa Hanson called just as I was heading out the door to do my run/walk. "There's a volleyball tournament in Yakima later this week," she said. "I want you to cover it."

"Yakima? That's two hours away."

"Mitch, you promised you'd cover volleyball. Chelsea Braker, Loaloa Toloto, and Terri Calvo are great hitters. Erica Stricker sets perfectly, and neither Marianne Flagler nor Rachel Black lets anything hit the ground. The team could make it to state."

"How about I interview the coach instead? It's Ms. Thomas, right? I could ask her some questions and then catch the home opener."

"Kimi's going."

"Kimi's going?"

"I knew that would change your mind. You've got a thing for Kimi, don't you?"

"I don't have a thing for Kimi."

"It's okay. She's cute, even if she is a little intense. And yes, she's going, which means you'll go, right?"

As soon as I said goodbye to Alyssa, I called Kimi. "It's great you're going to Yakima. When should I pick you up?"

There was a long silence. "That's nice of you, Mitch, but I'm going with Marianne and Rachel."

I felt like roadkill. "I guess I'll see you there," I managed.

"Yeah, sure." I was about to hang up when she spoke again. "Mitch, what about Angel? Have you got anything yet?"

"No, but I'll get something. It's just taking longer than I figured."

I said goodbye and cut the connection. What had I gotten myself into? A long, lonely drive to Yakima, that's what. And when I reached Yakima, how much time would I spend with Kimi? During the games, she'd be taking photos. Between games, she'd hang out with Marianne and Rachel.

I suddenly craved something sweet. I went outside, got in the Focus, and drove to Ballard Market. Once inside the store, I headed straight for the cookies. I found the Cougar Mountain section and pulled down a package of chocolate chip cookies. *One per day for eight days*—that's what I told myself. *Nothing wrong with that.*

I'd almost reached the checkout lady when I stepped back. Who was I kidding? I'd chow down those cookies like a dog chows down leftovers. I returned to the snack aisle, stuck the package back with his buddies, and beat it out of there.

In the car I felt oddly panicked, as if I were a heroin addict who'd turned down a fix. I had to do something positive, right then and there. I drove to the Locks, my eyes focused on the road as if I were an Indy 500 driver. I parked and, without bothering to stretch, started running. With every step, the panicky feeling faded.

Once I'd reached the Magnolia side, I decided to take a slightly different route. Instead of staying on Commodore Way, I headed up Elmore Street. I look back at that moment—at the turn—and I wonder why I made it, and what would have happened if I hadn't. Would everything have been different? Or was all that happened fated to happen?

Elmore Street is a hodge-podge. Eight buildings out of ten have signs like METAL FABRICATORS or SONAR EQUIPMENT— the men who work there are part of a world I know nothing about. Tucked among those buildings are older houses that have somehow dodged the wrecking ball. One in particular—2120 Elmore—caught my eye.

A gardener must have owned it long ago because the flowerbeds were filled with rosebushes. A few were in bloom, but most were scraggly-looking. I wondered if anyone still lived there. Just then a faded red Corolla pulled into the driveway. The passenger door swung open and out stepped a guy wearing a Philadelphia Eagles cap.

Angel Marichal.

I moved off the sidewalk and positioned myself behind a dumpster where I could see without being seen. As I watched, a man in his late twenties wearing a black leather jacket emerged from the driver's side—the same guy who'd been throwing with Angel before the first practice. They laughed as they bounded up the steps and into the house.

I was about to step back onto the sidewalk when the front door swung open and the two came back out, only now Angel carried a football. They crossed to an empty parking lot outside a shuttered marine electric company. Angel stood on one side; his friend stood about twenty-five yards away. Then Angel's rifle arm was on display again. He threw with such power and grace, it took my breath away. His partner's throws back to Angel were baby tosses in comparison. After a few minutes of catch, the older guy started running patterns—down-and-outs, up-and-ins. Angel hit him with laserlike precision.

They'd been playing catch for ten minutes when an old blue Cadillac turned right and headed straight toward the parking lot. Immediately both of them stopped and stared, like wild animals on alert. The older guy motioned for Angel to move behind one of the cars in the lot, and then reached into the inner pocket of his leather jacket and pulled something out. It gleamed silvery in the sunlight as he held it stiffly against his thigh. A gun? Was it a gun?

The Cadillac continued without slowing. The older guy watched intently until it was past. Only then did he put whatever it was back into his pocket. The two went back to football, but there were no smiles, no jokes. After a few tosses, they quit. As they returned to their house, I slipped away, down Elmore to Commodore Way.

Back home, as I showered before heading off to help with deliveries, I thought over what I'd seen. If it was a gun, what did it mean? And what should I do next? I turned off the water and stepped onto the bath mat.

Usually I flick off the light before I dry myself, but I'd been thinking so hard about the gun that I'd forgotten. That's why I caught a glimpse of myself in the mirror.

A tub of guts—that's what I was. A beached whale. I'd been exercising daily, but nobody would notice. Put a helicopter beanie on my head and I could pass for Twee-dledee.

I flicked off the light, dried myself, and dressed. Back in my room, I heard my cell phone beep, but I ignored it. I lay on my bed and stared at the ceiling, trying to erase the image of myself from my memory. The phone beeped again . . . and again. I flipped it open and saw *New Voice Message* on the screen. I hit *Listen* and put it to my ear.

"Mitch, it's me, Kimi. Ms. Thomas is making the players go together on the bus. So if the ride to Yakima is still open, I'll take it. Call me, okay?"

2

A WHOLE DAY WITH KIMI YON—or almost a whole day. She'd be on the sidelines during the games, but there'd be the ride to Yakima and the ride back. Ms. Thomas might want the team to eat together, which would mean Kimi might be with me for lunch and dinner. It was all too amazing.

I arranged to pick her up at six a.m. As soon as I pulled up in front of her house, her front door sprang open and she was out. She was wearing an orange hooded sweatshirt with the word *Princeton* across the front. I could see her talking over her shoulder to her dad as she ran down the walkway. She made it to the car so quickly that I never turned off the engine. "Go," she said, slamming the door.

We stopped at Peet's for coffee. I was about to tell her what I'd seen on Elmore Street, but she hunkered down inside her sweatshirt and made it clear that she didn't want to talk. That was okay. We had a long ride in front of us.

After Peet's, it was back in the car and up into the mountains, the sun rising in front of us, the sky pink and purple all around. I wanted to nudge her and say, *Look! Look!,* but she kept the hood of her sweatshirt pulled tightly around her face and slouched against the window, her eyes closed.

We'd gone about sixty miles and had reached the resorts at Snoqualmie Pass before Kimi finally roused. The amazing sky wasn't amazing anymore. "Do you ski?" she asked as she gazed out the window at the ski runs that scarred the mountainside.

I'd once had a nightmare where I slipped and fell down a steep slope during a snowstorm. I rolled all the way to the bottom, out of sight from the road. With my heavy coat and snow pants and boots, I couldn't get myself turned right. In the dream, I lay like a beetle on its back, my legs and arms waving helplessly, the snow falling and falling, burying me. "No," I said. "I've never learned. How about you?"

"A little."

That was it. Five minutes passed. Ten minutes. Fifteen. "Do you want to listen to music?" I asked.

She yawned. "That would be cool."

I had some jazz CDs in the backseat—Miles Davis and Dizzy Gillespie, stuff that was different and that I'd brought to impress her. Before I could reach for them, she pulled out her iPod, stuck the buds in her ears, put on sunglasses, and leaned against the window. She was gone then, her eyes closed, her music filling her world. Kimi

Yon was two feet from me, but she might as well have been two thousand miles away.

I hated Apple.

3

THE ARENA IN YAKIMA is called the SunDome, so I had it in my head that it would be open and airy. I couldn't have been more wrong. The sun doesn't penetrate concrete. Watching games inside the dome was like watching games at Home Depot.

Kimi roamed the sidelines, snapping photos, while I sat up in the bleachers, laptop open, trying to find something to write about. During the breaks—and there were lots of them—she hung out with Marianne and Rachel. They slouched in the corners of the gym, talking and eating. Kimi never once looked up at me.

Between matches I interviewed Ms. Thomas. *Great bunch of girls . . . one game at a time . . . important thing isn't wins and losses, it's playing the game right.*

The tournament dragged. I was lonely, and the excited cheers around me made me lonelier. I ate more than I should have—a hot dog, fries, and Coke at noon. Another combo at three thirty. A little before six o'clock, when the team had a ninety-minute break, Kimi walked out with Marianne, Rachel, and Erica Stricker. So much for eating dinner with her.

I slipped my laptop into its case and headed out. People might let me down, but food I could count on. Three blocks from the SunDome is a Mexican restaurant, Santiago's. A menu was taped to the window: enchiladas, tamales, chili con queso, fish tacos, flan, fried ice cream. I started to push the door open—and then changed my mind.

I walked up Yakima Avenue until the stores drifted away, turned, and came back on the other side of the street. There was nothing to see, but after all those hours in a hot gym, it felt good to move.

I stopped at a mom-and-pop grocery store and bought a peach yogurt, an apple, and a roll, all of which I ate while sitting on a bench in a tiny park on a side street. The yogurt was warm, the apple mushy, and the roll stale, but I felt good about my meal.

I returned to the SunDome for the trophy round of the tournament. Early in the day, when the Lincoln girls had been playing inferior opponents, they'd dominated. Terri Calvo, Loaloa Toloto, and Chelsea Braker were good. If a decent set came to any one of those three, she'd pound the ball down, making a kill. But against the better teams, Lincoln's flaws became glaring.

If a bump went wild or a set wasn't right, Chelsea, Loaloa, and Terri would look at one another, roll their eyes, and shake their heads. The other girls—Erica, Marianne, and Rachel—would glare right back. An earthquake fault ran right through the team. With a big lead, they were awesome. But in close games decided by a few rallies at the end—those they lost.

The real story would have been about the rift in the team, but no school newspaper prints negative stories about high school players. I slogged away on the preview article, pumping up their prospects, depressed because I knew what I was writing was neither true nor interesting. This kind of story wasn't why I ached to be a journalist.

Finally the awards were passed out—the Lincoln girls got ribbons for taking seventh—and the tournament was over. I expected nothing from Kimi on the ride back, and that's what I got. She scrunched down in her seat, wedged her backpack between her head and the window as if it were a pillow, leaned against it, and closed her eyes. Within ten minutes she was asleep. Thirty miles from Ellensburg, I called my mom, told her I was going to be really late, and then drove and drove.

When we exited the freeway, the change in speed woke Kimi. "Oh my God," she said. "What time is it?"

"Two," I answered.

She opened her cell phone and punched in a number. A second later she started talking. I couldn't understand a word, but I could figure out what she was saying. And I could figure out her father's angry replies, too.

From the freeway exit to her house takes about fifteen minutes. As soon as I pulled into her driveway, she swung the door open, jumped out of the car, and ran to the front door. It opened before she reached it.

I pulled the car door closed behind her. "You're welcome," I said to the empty seat, and I drove off.

4

THE NEXT MORNING, when I checked my e-mail, I saw that Kimi had sent me a dozen photos she'd taken at the tournament. I didn't bother to look. What did I care about her or her photos? I went down to the Locks and jogged over to Magnolia. But after my shower, I returned to her e-mail and opened the attachments, one by one.

All the photos were good, and one was flat-out great. She'd caught Erica Stricker, eyes closed, mouth tight, arms extended up and over the net, blocking a spike. It was exactly the type of photo the *Seattle Times* runs at the top of its prep sports page.

I stared at the photo on my computer screen. Kimi had treated me like a taxi driver. What did I owe her? Nothing. But I called her anyway.

"You really think the *Times* might use it?" she said, excited. "I wasn't sure if any were good enough for the *Lincoln Light*."

"For sure Alyssa will use them, but it can't hurt to try the *Times*."

"Should I e-mail it to them?"

My dad never used the phone if he was after a new client. *"They need to see you, Dan. That's the way of the world. Remember that."*

"No, Kimi. You should bring the photo to them yourself."

The line was quiet. "Will you go with me?"

Now it was my turn to let seconds silently tick away. I wanted to say that I had other things to do, but I didn't have to work until later, and I wanted to be with her more than I wanted to save my pride. "If you want."

Chet Jetton, known as Chet the Jet, is the high school sports editor at the *Seattle Times*. I thought we might have trouble getting to see him, but once the receptionist looked at Kimi's photo, she pointed us down a narrow aisle. "Turn right at the plastic tree. Chet's cubicle is the second one on the left. I'll buzz and tell him you're on your way."

Chet is fiftyish with a gray goatee. He was wearing a UW cap, a beat-up gray sweatshirt, and baggy jeans. He had his feet propped up on his desk and was leaning back in his chair, a pencil behind his ear, reading glasses down on his nose. He stood when he saw Kimi and introduced himself.

"So, Kimi, let me see your photo." Not once did he look at me, something that always seemed to happen when I was with Kimi.

Kimi handed it over. He scratched his chin. "We might be able to use it. We'll pay fifty dollars if we do. No guarantees, though."

"She needs to know now," I said, amazed by the firmness in my voice. "Otherwise we'll run it in the school newspaper."

Chet cocked his head and peered at me. "You her agent?"

"I'm the sports writer for the Lincoln Mustangs. I'll be sending you the game reports."

"You're my stringer?"

I nodded. "Mitch True," I said, sticking out my hand.

We shook. "Glad to meet you, Mitch." Then he turned back to Kimi's photo, tapping it with his finger. "We'll buy it," he said at last. "Ask the secretary for the forms for freelancers. Fill them out, mail them back, and you'll get your check for fifty dollars in a few weeks. You get a free-lance form too, Mitch."

"Will she get photo credit?" I asked.

"Of course she will," Chet snapped. "This is a professional newspaper. Nobody here will ever cheat you."

5

AS WE RETURNED TO THE FOCUS, Kimi's eyes were shining. "The *Seattle Times* took my photograph," she said over and over. "I can't believe it."

"It was a great photo."

She leaned over and kissed me on the cheek. "Thank you, Mitch. This wouldn't have happened without you."

It was a kiss she might give a brother, but it was a kiss. I tried not to turn red, which only made me turn redder. The anger I'd felt about the Yakima trip—it was gone. I started up the car and roared—if a Focus can roar—out of the parking lot. "Let's go to Peet's," I said. "My treat."

"I found out more about Angel," I said once we were seated upstairs looking out over Fremont Avenue. I was glad she'd picked the counter and not a table. I liked being near her, but sitting face-to-face made it harder for me to talk.

I described how I'd stumbled upon Angel's house and how I'd seen him throwing the football with his friend. "Then a car came up the block, moving fast. Angel hid while his friend stared down the car. I'm not completely sure about this, Kimi, but I think his friend pulled out a gun."

"You're joking."

"I know it sounds crazy, but I'm almost positive."

"When did this happen?"

"A few days ago."

"Why didn't you tell me sooner?" Her voice was miffed.

I shrugged. "I don't know. I guess I was waiting for a time when we could talk."

She stirred her latte for a moment, and then leaned toward me. "Actually, it fits with something I've been thinking," she said, her anger gone. "In fact, it fits perfectly."

A gun didn't fit with anything I'd been thinking. "Tell me."

"A few years ago, two cops went undercover at Federal Way High School. In February, they busted a dozen students for drugs, including three brothers who were running a meth lab in a shed behind their lawyer parents' fancy house, and a doctor's son who was selling stolen prescription pills. Lincoln has its share of druggies. They're buying meth and other stuff, which means somebody is selling. If the police department sent undercover agents into Federal Way High, they could do it at Lincoln High. I think Angel is a cop."

"A cop?"

"A cop."

The more I thought about it, the more possible it seemed. Kimi's theory explained why Angel looked so old, why his friend would have a gun. And Lincoln did have its share of drug users. Laurie Walloch and her friends for sure, and other kids I didn't know by name. A whole bunch of them had spooky eyes and looked wired twenty-four hours every day. But would the police bother with twenty or thirty kids?

"I can sort of see it," I said. "Only why would an undercover drug cop try out for the football team? Druggies aren't football players."

Kimi chewed on a fingernail for a bit. "Say I'm right and he's an undercover cop. What does he do? Show up the first day of school at Lincoln looking old and with no friends? How would he ever get in with anybody? But if he plays on the football team, when he shows up the first day, he's connected. The cops in Federal Way joined the yearbook staff. That gave them an excuse to go all through the school. Being a football player is like having a pass—football players can do what they want at school. Think about this, too. If Angel is an undercover cop, he'd want to be on the team, but he wouldn't want to be the star. That would attract too much attention. When he was throwing the football around with his friend, he didn't know we were watching, so he let his ability show. In front of McNulty, he pretends to be middling. It all fits with him being undercover, with staying under the radar."

She pursed her lips. "Mitch, if I'm right, if Angel is a cop, this could be a huge break for both of us. As he does his drug investigation, we investigate him. I get pictures; you write up how he gains the trust of the drug users. When the arrests come, we'll scoop everyone. The *Seattle Times* will run our story: 'Inside the Drug Bust at Lincoln High.' Both of our names will be on the front page. Think how much that would help our college applications."

6

I HELPED WITH MY PARENTS' afternoon deliveries, came home, ate dinner, and figured the day was done. Then, around eight thirty, my cell phone rang. Kimi was on the line. "You said you know where Angel lives. Let's go take some pictures."

"Now?"

"Why not?"

"What if he sees us? And what if it really was a gun?"

"You can park down the block. I'll use a telephoto lens; he won't notice anything. Anyway, cops don't shoot people for sitting in a car."

Five minutes later, I pulled up in front of Kimi's house. She hurried down her walkway, wearing shorts and a pink top, camera bag slung over her shoulder, her father at the door watching.

I drove across the Ballard Bridge, wound past Fishermen's Terminal, and made a right onto Commodore Way. I turned left on Elmore Street, drove one hundred feet up the block, pulled to the curb, and stopped. I flicked off the headlights but kept the engine idling. "There," I said, pointing up the block and across the street. "The one with the bars on the windows."

Kimi started snapping pictures of the ramshackle house.

"Isn't it too dark?" I asked.

"The twilight will give the photos a mysterious look. I can use Photoshop to brighten the images if I need to."

With every click of the camera, the whole undertaking felt increasingly dangerous, but Kimi kept snapping away.

At last she put the lens cap on the camera and stuck the camera back into its case. I was about to speed off when she leaned forward, her brow furrowed, and nodded toward the house. "Wait. Do you notice something odd about the iron bars on the windows and doors?"

I looked. "Not really."

"The paint is peeling; the porch looks like it could crumble away, but the bars are brand new. And see how fancy they are? My dad recently had security bars put over the windows on our house. Wrought iron like that costs money." She turned to me. "I bet there's a top-notch security system in place."

"And all that means?"

"The ramshackle house is a cover. If you look quickly, it seems like one thing; look harder, and it's something else. The same with Angel."

That moment the front door opened and the older guy, wearing his Seahawks sweatshirt, stepped onto the porch. He looked down the block opposite from us, and then he turned and stared at the Focus. "Get down," I ordered, and we both slunk down in the seat.

For a long moment, we stayed down. Then a new dread came over me. The Focus's engine was running. Had the guy heard it? What if he was walking toward the car right at this moment? What if he had a gun in his hand?

I inched my head up until I was able to see. The guy was coming toward us, and fast. I didn't wait to see what he wanted. I threw the Focus into drive and peeled out of there. "Stay down!" I barked at Kimi. As I tore past the guy, I put my hand up by the side of my face so he couldn't see me. At the end of the block I made a hard left and then raced through the side streets of lower Magnolia until I reached Dravus Street, which I followed down to Elliott Avenue. Neither Kimi nor I said a word until I pulled up in front of her house and killed the engine.

"My heart is pounding so hard I can hear it," she said.

"Mine, too."

I looked at her, and for no reason we both started to laugh.

Her porch light flicked on. "I better get inside," she said, the laughter subsiding as quickly as it had come, and she was out the door and up the walkway.

I headed toward my home, but turned north on Thirty-second and drove up to Sunset Hill Park instead. I parked, walked to the chain-link fence, and looked out over Puget Sound. Two ferries glided on the water, their lights twinkling in the black.

I tried to make sense of what had happened. I'd completely panicked, that I knew for sure. But everything else was murky. Had the guy really been coming toward us? Or was he just going for a walk?

I stared at Puget Sound for a while, my mind rolling like the waves, and then drove home. All night I kept waking up, then falling back asleep. I'd finally fallen into a deep sleep when my cell phone rang. It was eight in the morning, and it was summer, yet Alyssa was wide awake. "How are your football stories going?" she asked. "I'd like two, you know. A preview, and then a story about the game against Mater Dei on Saturday. Oh, and a volleyball preview, too."

"I'll have them all by next week," I said, my mind foggy.

"If you did the previews early, we could get the pages ready for publication. I want to have the September issue out as soon as possible, maybe even the first day."

"I'll get it to you as soon as I can, Alyssa."

The volleyball preview was done, but the football preview was causing me nothing but trouble. For a solid hour I worked on it. I must have tried fifteen different hooks, but none worked. I'd write a few paragraphs only to have my ideas dwindle away. The whole time I was wasting my effort on those useless paragraphs, I could feel an imp sitting on my shoulder. *"Horst! Horst!"* the rascal kept whispering in my ear. *"Write about Horst!"* Finally I gave in, and once I focused on Horst, the article wrote itself.

7

THE HIGH SCHOOL FOOTBALL SEASON in Seattle opens every year with the Seattle Challenge. Powerhouse teams from California fly up to square off against the best Puget Sound teams at Qwest Field, the Seahawks stadium. Because of Horst's growing reputation, Lincoln High had been invited, and we were matched against Mater Dei, a football factory from Southern California.

The morning of the game, my mom stopped me as I headed out the door for my run/walk. "You look slimmer, Dan." I grimaced, because I hate it when anyone says anything about my body, but she persisted. "Really, there's a change."

"You look taller, too," my dad called out. "I told you you'd grow."

I drove to the Locks, but before starting my run, I looked at my face in the rearview mirror. Were they right? Or did I still look like Wilbur from *Charlotte's Web*, which is how Heather Lowry had described me in eighth grade.

I could still picture her: blond, curly-haired, with her wicked smile.

I stepped out of the car, not sure that my face looked thinner, not sure that my legs were longer, but hopeful. Then I went for my run. Each day I was running more and walking less; I could actually imagine a day when I'd run the whole way.

When I finished, I returned home and showered. I was done working—school was starting soon, and my parents gave me the last week of summer off—but having nothing to do made me restless. I cleaned my closet and straightened up my desk. At three I called Kimi and asked if she needed a ride, but she was going with Marianne and Rachel, which is what I'd expected.

Kickoff was at seven thirty, so I left at six thirty. As I drove, I kept changing channels on the radio. I was glad I didn't have any junk food in the car, because when I'm nervous, I eat. A mile from the stadium I panicked, certain I'd left my press pass at home on the kitchen table. I pulled my wallet out and rifled through it, my eyes darting back and forth from the road to the contents until I discovered the pass behind my driver's license.

I found a parking spot four blocks south of the stadium. I showed my pass at the press gate, and the usher waved me through. As I shoved the pass back into my wallet, I spotted Chet the Jet and my shoulders slumped. "Don't look so happy to see me," he said, smiling wryly. "And relax. This will be my only Lincoln game. You'll get plenty of chances to be my stringer."

I managed a weak smile. "I don't mind that you're here."

He shook his head. "We both know the score. Since I'm here, you get no byline. It's good to be greedy for a byline—greed is a quality every top-notch reporter has in abundance. And I'm sure there's room for fifty bucks in your wallet."

He moved toward the press box. I could have followed him; my press pass would have gotten me inside. Mr. Dewey had told us that the press box at Qwest had computer terminals and free food, but he'd also said that behind the one-inch pane of glass, reporters never cheered, no matter how exciting the play on the field. "Cheering is considered unprofessional," Dewey had said, "like an undertaker telling jokes at a funeral."

I worked my way to section 109, right on the fifty-yard line. I'd have to sit toward the top, in the shaded area, to see the words I typed on my laptop. I started trudging up the stairs, but had gone only a few steps when Britt Lind stepped out into the aisle, smiled, and said hello.

Britt is Horst's girlfriend. Green eyes, sandy blond hair, a body that Noah Webster could use to illustrate the word *voluptuous*. I looked left; I looked right. I looked behind me. Was Britt Lind talking to me?

"Hi, Britt," I said.

Her gaze fell on my laptop case, and I understood. "You're the sportswriter this year, right?" She flashed another smile. "Make sure you get down the great things Horst does."

"If Horst does great things, I'll write them down."

She tossed her head back like a thoroughbred before the Kentucky Derby. "Oh, he'll do great things. He always does. He's great at everything."

I nodded, and then climbed ten rows and settled into my seat.

8

QWEST FIELD HOLDS 65,000 PEOPLE. About 10,000 were at the game—a big crowd for a high school football game in Seattle, but the size of the stadium made the crowd seem small. I scanned the sidelines with my binoculars until I found Kimi. She was wearing a long-sleeved shirt with the word *Mustangs* running down both sleeves. She paced up and down the sideline, snapping shot after shot.

Mater Dei has one of the great high school football programs in the country. A slew of NFL players have come from there, including two Heisman Trophy winners. But Lincoln had a chance. The newspapers in Southern California were predicting a down year for the Monarchs— too many freshmen at too many key positions. Playing in front of a hostile crowd more than a thousand miles from home, those kids would be scared.

The Lincoln band played the national anthem. The crowd cheeered, and then I sat down, opened my laptop, and stared at the blank screen. McNulty had told me that I had to focus on Horst, and I'd said I would, but McNulty wasn't leaning over my shoulder now. I could write what I wanted, and Alyssa would print what I wrote. If Angel played the way I knew he could, then his name would appear prominently in my article.

We won the coin toss. Blake Stein took the kickoff and plowed straight upfield to the thirty-five. Lincoln's offense stormed onto the field, guys pounding one another's shoulder pads and hopping up and down like jack-in-the-boxes.

Horst was sensational on the opening drive, marching Lincoln right down the field. Ten yards on a toss sweep;

twelve on a screen pass; eight on a simple in. The scoring play came on a bomb down the sideline to a streaking Coby Eliot—a gorgeous touchdown pass to end a perfect drive. It all happened so fast, I had trouble keeping up with my notes.

After the kickoff Mater Dei's offense took the field, but McNulty had his defense huddle around him. Finally they broke and hustled to the line of scrimmage. The program said Angel Marichal was wearing forty-four. I had my binoculars on the players, searching for him. Where would McNulty put him? Defensive end . . . linebacker . . . strong safety? A guy with Angel's size and speed could play almost anywhere.

I hunted, and then hunted some more; he wasn't on the field. I turned my binoculars to the sidelines. Still I had trouble finding him. Finally I spotted him at the far end of the bench, sitting off by himself, ten yards from anyone.

It made no sense. There'd been two weeks of practice. McNulty wanted to win, and he wanted to win badly. Even if Angel didn't star during drills, his size, speed, and strength should have gotten him a starting spot some-where on the defense. And why was Angel putting a wall between himself and his teammates?

I looked down on the field for Kimi. Every once in a while she'd train her camera on Angel and snap a few photos before turning back to the action on the field. What did she make of it?

I wanted to puzzle it out, or at least try to, but I had a game to cover. My eyes went back to the field. McNulty had pushed eight defenders up close, daring Mater Dei to pass. The Monarchs' coach didn't run the risk, running two dive plays that moved the ball to the twenty-one. On third and four, McNulty blitzed Darren Clarke, the middle linebacker. The Mater Dei quarterback—a sophomore named Hunter Ford—sailed his pass over his receiver's head and into the arms of one of our safeties, who returned the interception to the fifteen-yard line before he was forced out of bounds.

About ninety-nine percent of the crowd were Lincoln fans, and they were up cheering as Horst took his position under center. He dropped back as if to pass, but then tucked the ball under his arm and raced upfield on a quarterback draw. At the five he straight-armed a Monarch linebacker to the ground. Two guys hit him near the goal line, but he carried both of them into the end zone. Touchdown Lincoln.

The Lincoln players in the end zone were jumping around. So were the players on the sideline: jumping and pounding on one another, flirting with an unsportsman-like conduct penalty by spilling onto the field. All except

Angel. He had his helmet raised high, and he was shaking it, but he didn't join any of the clumps of celebrating players.

Mater Dei fought back. On their next possession, the Monarchs drove the ball the length of the field. They'd have scored a touchdown if their receiver hadn't dropped a pass in the end zone. As it was, their field goal kicker split the uprights from thirty yards, cutting the lead to 13–3.

After that score, the game became a defensive struggle: Mater Dei would make a few first downs, then punt. We'd gain twenty or thirty yards, always because of Horst, but then there'd be a penalty or a dropped pass, and we'd have to punt. Subs came in on offense and defense, giving starters a blow. The entire second string rotated in for one full drive. I kept waiting for Angel to take the field, but McNulty never called his number.

It looked like neither team would score again before the break. Then, with a minute remaining in the half, Mater Dei's wide receiver caught a simple slant pass, broke Darren Clarke's tackle, and he was gone, racing seventy-three yards for a touchdown. The point after made the score 13–10, and around me it was so quiet that every cough echoed through the stands. After a couple more plays, the horn sounded and the players trotted off the field to the locker rooms.

I spent halftime checking the notes I'd taken on my laptop. I wouldn't be writing a recap for the *Times,* but Alyssa was giving me two hundred words in the *Lincoln Light.* When I looked over what I had, I saw it was a rerun of the three previous years. Horst, Horst, and more Horst—exactly what McNulty had predicted.

Mater Dei came out running an option attack, something they hadn't shown at all in the first half. After their quarterback took the snap, he'd work his way down the line of scrimmage, feeling out the defense. Sometimes he'd find a hole and snake through it. More often, he'd hold the ball until he was about to be tackled, then pitch out to the tailback. And what a tailback. The Mater Dei coach hadn't played him much in the first half, going with a power runner instead.

The program said the guy's name was Marcus Bintz, and he was rocket-fast. Once he had the ball he'd race for the corner, all the while looking to cut back against the grain. When he found a spot—*boom!*—he hit the hole hard, piling up yards that eventually turned into touchdowns.

Bintz would have blown us out if Horst hadn't matched him play for play. Time after time, Horst would dodge blitzing linebackers until he spotted an open receiver. And then the ball was gone, out of his hand in a millisecond. Nearly every pass hit a receiver right on the numbers. If he did misfire, Lenny Westwood or Coby Eliot would bail him out with leaping catches. The game was like one of those old Ali–Frazier fights they show on ESPN—Bintz and Horst traded blow after blow, but neither would crumble.

All we needed was one stop, but Darren Clarke was being eaten alive by Mater Dei. He didn't have the quickness to move down the line as the option play developed. When Bintz cut back against the grain, Clarke was too tired to do anything but reach out with an arm, and Bintz wasn't going down unless somebody laid a hit on him.

It was baffling. There sat Angel, off by himself at the end of the bench. Had McNulty forgotten about him? How does a high school football coach forget six foot three and 220 pounds of muscle in a game where his team is being outmuscled?

We were up by a field goal when Horst made his first and only terrible pass. It was third and eight, late in the fourth quarter. He was rolling to his right, the defense chasing him. All his receivers were covered, so he turned and threw back across his body into the center of the field. The ball wobbled in the air, and a Mater Dei linebacker picked it off. He had a clear field in front of him and a ten-yard lead on everyone else. I thought he was gone; everybody thought he was gone. Somehow Horst chased that linebacker down and tackled him, but not until the Mater Dei guy had made it to Lincoln's twenty-one-yard line.

Mater Dei's offense raced onto the field, pumped to steal the game. On first down, Marcus Bintz took the option pitch and beat everyone to the corner—an eight-yard gain. On second and two, Bintz cut his run back against the flow for seven more. If he hadn't tripped, he'd have scored. Still, Mater Dei had a first down and goal on the six.

Two minutes remained in the game. We were up by three, but we hadn't stopped Bintz before. Why would we be able to stop him now?

McNulty called time and had the defense huddle around him. What could he say that would rally them? The ref blew his whistle, the huddle broke, and the players trotted back to their positions. I sat bolt upright in my seat. Darren Clarke was out. Forty-four was lined up at middle linebacker.

Angel Marichal was finally in the game.

Mater Dei came up to the line. The QB took the snap, faked a handoff to his fullback, and started down the line, waiting, waiting. Finally he made the pitch. Bintz took the ball and headed for the corner, but Angel shed his blocker and drove his shoulder into Bintz, knocking him backwards.

Loss of two.

Clock running.

On second and goal the fullback took the quick handoff and drove into the middle. Angel was there again, stuffing him for absolutely no gain. And when Angel stood, he started flapping his arms, calling for noise from the crowd, pumping up his teammates. This from the guy who'd sat alone and silent for two hours.

Third and goal, with just over a minute left.

Mater Dei hustled to the line of scrimmage. I thought they'd go back to Bintz, and they did, setting up a screen pass for him. Angel read it from the start and dropped into the flat. The quarterback threw the ball anyway, and Angel jumped the route, stretched out, and snagged the ball. He took one step, cradled the ball in both arms, and then fell to the ground, protecting the interception.

The game was ours.

Mater Dei had no time-outs left. Horst took a knee, and then another one, and then 10,000 people roared as the clock went to 00:00. Lincoln High had beaten Mater Dei.

9

AFTER THE GAME, I quickly worked my way down to the field. As soon as Kimi saw me, she rushed over. "He's no senior." The words came out fast. "He's a grown man. The close-ups I shot of his face prove it, too. He's got to be a cop. Why else would an adult be in a high school? Come on." And then she was off, before I could say a word, heading into the bowels of the stadium.

"Where are we going?" I called out as I broke into a trot to catch up.

"To interview him."

"But McNulty said no."

"That was *before*," she said. "He can't turn us down now that Angel has saved the game."

We worked our way to the door leading to the locker rooms. Kimi stepped back then and gave me a push. I stood tall, sucked in my gut, and knocked hard on the door. After a minute it opened. "I'd like to interview Angel Marichal," I said, flashing my press pass.

The security cop—a giant of a guy who could have been a poster boy for LA Fitness—looked at me as if I were a fly that might not be worth swatting. "You from a newspaper?"

"The *Lincoln Light*," I answered.

"What is that? A school newspaper?"

"Does that matter?" Kimi said.

He looked past me to Kimi, and the edge in his voice softened.

"Wait here."

We stood for five minutes before the door reopened.

"Coach McNulty said no," the guy said, looking only at Kimi. "I'm sorry."

As we walked together out of the stadium, Kimi called Marianne. "Where are you? . . . No, don't come back. I'll take the bus . . . Yeah, see you tomorrow."

"You don't have to take the bus," I said. "I can give you a ride."

"You sure?"

"Sure, I'm sure. We could go to Peet's if you want."

"That sounds good."

Twenty minutes later we were sitting side by side at the upstairs counter—what I was starting to think of as *our* counter. Kimi was glum, so I asked her to show me her game photos. She held her camera so that I could see. Lots of her photos were great, but the best was a shot of Angel, arms fully extended, making his interception, controlling the football with the very tips of his fingers. "Let's e-mail that one to Chet," I said.

She shook her head. "There's no point. The *Times* had a photographer at the game."

"I'll bet he didn't get a shot half as good as that."

"He was there, Mitch. They won't print anything of mine. You know that."

Sunday morning I checked out the online edition of the *Seattle Times*. The headline read Lincoln Stuns California

POWERHOUSE. In the right-hand corner was a photo of Horst Diamond unleashing a pass. I read Chet the Jet's article, expecting all the time that the next sentence would detail Angel's last-minute heroics. At the tail end, Chet wrote, "A late interception sealed the victory." And that was it. No name, no description of the incredible plays Angel had made on the previous downs.

It was poor writing. Chet the Jet should have led with Angel's plays as a hook, and then gone to Horst Diamond. My cell rang. "Have you seen the article in the *Times*?" Kimi asked.

"I just finished reading it and I don't get it. The only explanation is that he left early and didn't see Angel's interception."

There was a pause. "I have another idea," Kimi said.

"What?"

"Maybe Chet knows Angel is a cop. Maybe he's in on the scheme. Maybe McNulty told him he had to keep Angel's name out of the paper."

She was talking so fast, I was having trouble keeping up. "You think McNulty knows?"

"Think about it, Mitch. A policeman couldn't infiltrate a school without help. The undercover cops in Federal Way hung out with drug dealers for months before they made their arrests. The principal knew they were cops, and so did some of the teachers. If Angel is undercover, he'd have

the same kind of support. McNulty . . . the principal . . .
the teachers—they'd all have to know."

"You're pretty sure you're right about this, aren't you?"

"Only sort of sure, but I'm clueless about what to
do next."

"That makes two of us."

10

I SAID GOODBYE, closed up my cell, and then opened my
laptop and got to work. Chet the Jet had written a mediocre story for the *Times*; I was going to write a better one
for the *Lincoln Light*.

I had less than a page to describe forty-eight minutes
of football, but lack of space wasn't my main problem.
The final score would be in the headline, so there'd be no
suspense. Somehow, I had to capture my readers—and
that made my first sentence crucial. I typed, deleted,
typed some more, deleted some more, thought for a while,
typed, and then stopped and read over what I had.

**In a game in which sixty-five points were scored,
it took the last-minute defensive heroics of
newcomer Angel Marichal to preserve Lincoln's**

stunning upset victory over Mater Dei at Qwest Field in the season opener.

A little wordy, but acceptable. I moved on.

My next one hundred and fifty words recounted the accomplishments of Horst and Lenny Westwood and the other offensive players. I threw in a sentence on Marcus Bintz just to be fair. I closed by returning to my opening, but adding more bang, just like Mr. Dewey had taught me.

With an offense clicking under Horst Diamond's leadership and a defense strengthened by Angel Marichal, this year's Lincoln Mustangs have a chance to stampede all the way to the state title game in Tacoma.

I read the article over, made a few small changes, and then called Alyssa. "I've got both the preview and the recap finished. I'll e-mail them to you."

"That's great." I could almost feel her smile. "Mitch, I'll be working in the newspaper room at school all day tomorrow. Any chance you could help out?"

"Tomorrow? Tomorrow is Labor Day. How are you going to get in?"

"Teachers will be there."

■ ■ ■ ■

She was right. The next morning the main doors to Lincoln were all open; at least a dozen teachers were in their classrooms working. It turned out that Alyssa had gotten nearly everyone on the staff to write something. I spent the day helping her format pages, and then I drove her to the printer in Pioneer Square, south of downtown.

Tuesday I drove back to Pioneer Square with Alyssa. We picked up the newspapers and took them to Lincoln High. She kept the first ten copies for herself, slipping them into a manila envelope so they wouldn't get wrinkled. Then we went from entrance to entrance, filling each rack.

"You know something, Alyssa," I said when we finished. "I bet this is the first time a newspaper has been printed and ready to go on the first day of school. And I don't mean just at Lincoln. I mean at any high school. What you've done is amazing."

She turned to me. "Thank you, Mitch. You don't know how much that means to me." And then she hugged me.

I didn't know what to do, so I wrapped my arms around her, not daring to squeeze for fear she'd think I was a pervert. I was sure she'd pull away, but instead she started sobbing, and she kept crying, so I finally did give her a squeeze, and she squeezed back, and I decided that having a real live girl in my arms was definitely an okay thing, and that doing it on a regular basis would also definitely be an okay thing. Finally Alyssa stepped back and wiped her eyes with her sleeve. "I'm sorry. I don't know what's wrong with me. I guess I'm just really, really tired." She snuffled once, and then she patted me on the chest. "You're a good guy, Mitch True."

I did my run/walk soon after I got home. As I plodded along, I thought about Alyssa. Since newspaper is just an after-school club at Lincoln, nobody has to write anything. If I'd been elected editor, I'd have been lucky to squeeze out enough stories for two or three newspapers over the course of the year. Alyssa might not manage to print one every month, like she hoped, but she'd come close. I hadn't been cheated out of the editorship; she'd been the better choice all along.

PART THREE

I

SCHOOL STARTED THE NEXT DAY. Wherever kids filed into the hallways, a stack of *Lincoln Light*s waited for them. I watched as student after student grabbed one, flipped through it quickly, and then stuffed it into a backpack.

When the warning bell rang, I headed off to AP English. I'd had Mr. Kelly before, so there was nothing surprising. In fact, there was nothing surprising in any of my morning classes. I got the books, got the syllabi, and heard the same warnings about keeping up with the work. *One more year,* I thought, *and I'm out of here.* The only good thing was watching kids sneak-read the *Lincoln Light.* Alyssa had been right; it was the sports page that most people turned to.

Finally it was lunch. I headed to the commons, where I bought a small deli sandwich and a vanilla yogurt. Then I looked around for someplace to sit.

For the three years I'd been at Lincoln, I'd eaten in an alcove around the corner from the main room. Other guys ate there, too. Toby, who was a chess genius; Lars, who played the flute; Michael, who was deep into alternate reality games. I suppose they were my friends, though it was only at lunch that we were together.

Out of habit, I started for the alcove, but then I stopped. I was a senior now, not a freshman, and I was trying to make myself into a different person. I spotted a nearly empty table toward the center of the cafeteria and plunked myself down.

Within minutes, kids sat down around me. They nodded and I nodded back. Once in a while someone asked me something. No big conversation or anything, just the usual: *What do your classes look like, Mitch?* I answered, asked the same question of them, they answered, and it was okay.

About ten minutes before fifth period started, I spotted Kimi standing by the juice machine frantically motioning for me to join her. "See you around," I said to the kids at the table. Then I bussed my tray and walked over to her.

"Did you see the newspaper?" I said when I'd reached her. "Your pictures came out great. Everybody was looking at them."

"Yeah, yeah. I saw them. Look, Mitch—way in the back corner. That's Angel, isn't it?"

I followed Kimi's eyes. "That's him."

"Do you see who he's with? They're all the druggies."

About twenty-five kids were in the corner where Angel was eating. There had always been twenty-five there, from day one of my freshman year. The only two I knew were Laurie Walloch and Lynn Anderson. In grade school both of them had been seminormal, but by middle school they started getting into purple hair, body piercings, tattoos, drugs, alcohol, and more drugs.

Kimi and I pretended to talk, but really we took turns checking out the action at Laurie and Lynn's table. I figured that if Angel really was an undercover cop, he'd strike up a conversation with one of the druggies near him, but he kept his head down and his mouth shut. Finally he got up, dumped his trash, and headed out the back door into the courtyard.

Kimi watched him leave, and then turned to me. "If you wanted to buy drugs, where would you go?"

"What?" I said, startled by the question.

"There must be some street corner or park where dealers hang out, don't you think?"

"Yeah, probably. Why?"

"Because if Angel starts hanging out at one of those places, that would be more evidence that he's an undercover cop. You see what I mean?"

I nodded. "Yeah, I do. And I know somebody who can answer your question."

Austin Goldman and I had gone to elementary school together, and he was one of the guys who'd sat down at the lunch table with me. Goldman's father was a public defender, which meant he had to handle drug cases.

The afternoon classes were just like the morning ones. When the final bell rang, I hustled out of class so I could get to the front steps of Lincoln before many kids had left. I wasn't there long when Austin pushed the door open and started down the stairs.

"Austin," I called, waving to him. "You got a minute?"

His eyebrows went up in surprise, but he came over. "What's up, Mitch?"

"This is going to sound strange, but if a guy was going to score some drugs, where would he go?"

He lowered his voice and looked around. "Mitch, you aren't into drugs, are you?"

"No, no. Not me. I'm working on an article about drug use at Lincoln."

His face relaxed. "I couldn't picture you as a user."

"So, can you help me out?"

He scratched the back of his neck. "Well, my dad's always warning me to stay clear of the Moonlite Mini-Mart up on Eighty-fifth, the one next to the strip club. So if I was looking for some serious drugs, that's where I'd go."

"Thanks. Thanks a lot," I said.

I started off, but before I'd taken two steps, Austin grabbed my arm. "Mitch, you don't want to go there. Last June a guy got shot in the parking lot, and just last month two people got stabbed."

That night I called Kimi. "How about if we go Friday night and check it out?" she said.

She was moving faster than I wanted. "I was thinking we'd just scope things out at school for a month. Watch Angel and see what happens. If he starts trying to fit in with Laurie Walloch and all them, then we'd go to the Moonlite Mini-Mart."

"I don't want to wait, Mitch. If he's a cop, we'll have to go up there a bunch of times anyway. I'll need pictures and you'll need to flesh out your story. The sooner we start, the better."

"Austin said the place is dangerous."

"We can park across from the mini-mart and check out what happens from there. It'll be like a stakeout."

"When we did that at Angel's house, it didn't work out so well."

"Come on, Mitch. Nothing happened to us. Anyway, Elmore Street was deserted. This time we'll be on Eighty-fifth. Cars will be streaming by in every direction."

2

I PICKED KIMI UP at nine on Friday night and we drove to Eighty-fifth and Fifteenth. I parked and cut the engine. The Moonlite Mini-Mart and the strip club next to it were seedy in the daytime and even seedier at night. Cars were all around us, but they were speeding by, making it a busy yet lonely spot. It would have been great to be sitting with Kimi if it weren't for the hard knot of fear in my stomach. "You sure about this?" I said after a few minutes.

"We're totally safe," she said, but I heard doubt in her voice.

The parking lot buzzed with activity. Most of the people were shoppers who'd head into the mini-mart to pick up milk or potato chips or beer and then drive away. Outside the store were a handful of guys leaning against the wall, smoking. Every once in a while a car would pull up, a window would roll down, and one of the guys would drift over to the car. Whenever that happened, Kimi aimed her camera and snapped a photo. I could never actually see the exchange of money for drugs—a hand would go into the car and then come out—but it was obvious what was happening. A gold Mercury Cougar with tinted windows pulled in and out of the parking lot four times in thirty minutes.

As the minutes passed, the knot in my stomach loosened. Sitting next to Kimi, talking to her while she took photos of what was going on across the street—it was a little like being at a game, where you see what is happening, but you are outside the action.

We'd been waiting for over an hour when Kimi suddenly pointed. "Mitch, look! Is that him? Is that Angel?"

She handed me her camera and I used the zoom to get a closer look. As I watched, the guy walked across the lot, took a spot against the wall, lit a cigarette, and then stood there, his eyes down. "Maybe," I said. "It's too dark to be sure."

"Go buy something, Mitch. When you're walking through the parking lot, take a close look."

The fear rushed back. The Focus was safe. I had the key in the ignition; I had three feet of clearance in front of me. In ten seconds, I could start the car and be out of there. What Kimi wanted me to do—poke my nose into a circle of drug dealers—wasn't safe. If it had been anybody other than Kimi who was asking, I wouldn't have gone. But it *was* Kimi who was asking.

I got out—mouth dry as dust—locked the door, and walked to the corner. I waited awhile before the light turned green. I tried to look casual as I crossed the street, but my legs felt as if they were made of rubber.

I made my way through the parking lot of the mini-mart, entered the store, bought a pack of gum, and headed out. I glanced over toward the guys leaning against the wall, but the Angel-guy had his back to me. I crumpled up the gum wrapper and sauntered over to the garbage can. I tossed the wrapper into the trash, turned, and got a clear look—the guy by the telephone booth was at least twenty years older than Angel.

Instantly my heart rate slowed. I walked through the parking lot, again waited for the light to change, and then headed for the Focus. When I was about thirty feet away, I made eye contact with Kimi and smiled. I'd done it. But instead of smiling back, her eyes widened in fear. That's when I felt hands grab me.

There were two of them. They lifted me up, carried me to the Focus, and spun me around. They looked like Hells Angels—black shirts; long, stringy hair; huge tattooed arms; mean eyes. "What are you doing?" the one on the left growled.

"What do you mean?" I said, my voice shaky.

"Your girlfriend has been taking pictures for the last hour. What's she taking pictures of, fat boy?"

"She's not taking pictures of anything."

"Give me the keys. I want her camera."

The other guy started pounding on the windshield. "Put the phone down, bitch!"

I looked over my shoulder. Kimi was punching numbers into her cell.

"Give me the keys, you fat turd," my guy screamed, and he slammed me against the car. My spine hit the door handle hard, and I cried out in pain.

I had the keys clenched tightly in my hand. I couldn't let them get at Kimi. They'd slap her around, take her camera, hurt her.

"The keys!" He pushed me hard against the car a second time and then put his forearm under my throat. "You give me those keys, or I'm going to pound my fist into that tub of guts until you puke blood."

His partner was still pounding on the windshield. "Put the phone down, and give me that camera. Now!"

Kimi, behind the thin layer of glass, was hunched down, her shoulders shaking, her mouth up against the cell phone. I looked toward the street. Cars were zipping past in both directions. Why didn't anybody help us?

The guy hit me hard in the stomach. Pain shot through me, and then he hit me again. I couldn't breathe; his forearm was choking me. I felt like I was going to puke up my guts. "Those were baby taps," he said, his voice evil. "Want to feel the real thing?"

Tears welled in my eyes. I shook my head. "Stop." I said, gasping.

"The keys!"

I wanted to sacrifice myself to keep Kimi safe. That's what I wanted to do. But I saw his hand form another fist, and fear took over every cell in my body. I let my fingers relax; the keys clattered to the street.

He smirked as he reached down to pick them up. Just then a police cruiser turned left from Fifteenth onto Eighty-fifth, siren roaring. In a flash both attackers were gone, tearing down the alley like rats.

The door to the police car opened and the cop—an old guy—emerged. He flashed his light at Kimi, still hunched over, and then he turned it on me. "You okay?" the cop asked. "They steal anything?"

"I'm okay," I said. "They were after her camera, but they didn't get anything."

He looked at Kimi, who was now sitting up, and then back to me. "What are you two doing here? This isn't a place to hang out."

"We're reporters," I said, then added, "for our school newspaper. We're writing a story about drugs and—"

"Kid," he said, his face filled with disgust, "let the police take care of that, okay? We don't need you and your little girlfriend out here making our job harder. Now get going, and stay gone."

"Yes, sir," I said.

As he headed back to his cruiser, I retrieved the keys from the street, opened the car door, and slid into the seat. Without looking at Kimi, I started the engine and drove off.

I drove to Green Lake and parked in the lot by the rowing center. As soon as I shut off the engine, Kimi leaned her head against my shoulder and sobbed. I had a big lump in my throat, too, and my ribs ached. "It's okay," I managed. "It's okay."

We sat like that for a few minutes. Then she took some Kleenex out of her purse and wiped her eyes. "Was it Angel?"

I shook my head. "The guy was way older."

"You were so brave. I heard him screaming at you. I saw him beating you. I should have just given them my camera. I don't know why I didn't. I'm sorry."

I didn't answer. What could I say? She didn't know I'd let the keys drop out of my hand. She had no idea that they were fifteen seconds from being inside the car, from grabbing the camera from her, from having their hands all over her.

I drove her home. After she got out of the car, she turned back to me. "I don't want to do this anymore, Mitch. It's too scary. I'm finished." She closed the car door and hurried into her house. Once she was safely inside, I drove home and parked in my driveway. My gut hurt so much that I didn't even want to move, so instead of going into the house, I sat in the silent car.

I'm not the kind of person who will ever make news. I'm too ordinary, and I've known that for as long as I can remember. That's why the movie about Nixon had been such a big deal to me. I could picture myself being like those reporters. I could scratch at a story until I got to the bottom of it. The newsmen in Afghanistan and Iraq didn't charge into battle firing guns. They carried cameras and tape recorders and paper and pencils. Those were the tools they used to shine light into the darkness. I'd thought that someday I'd be brave like them. But tonight I hadn't had the courage to keep my fist clenched around a set of keys.

3

THERE WAS A FOOTBALL GAME the next night against Roosevelt High. My ribs still ached and I didn't feel like doing anything, but around noon I got an e-mail from Chet the Jet. *I'll be covering the Bellevue–Skyline game,* he wrote, *so you'll be my eyes. One hundred words and an accompanying photo by midnight. Fifty bucks for you and fifty more for your photographer.*

Game time was seven, so around six I drove to broken-down Memorial Stadium, Lincoln's home field, and found a seat on the fifty-yard line. A little later I spotted Kimi along the sidelines, camera bag over her shoulder. I waved to her; she waved back, and then she turned away.

I wanted to put Angel out of my mind, but throughout the game it was as if my head were on a swivel. I watched the plays on the field, watched Lincoln shut down Roosevelt, watched Horst complete pass after pass, watched all that and somehow watched Angel, too, sitting alone at the end of the bench.

He did play some. He was on the field for kickoffs, punts, and extra points. And right before halftime, Coach McNulty gave him one series at linebacker. For those three plays he dominated the field, shedding blockers and annihilating running backs. Roosevelt began that possession with first and ten on the thirty-one. By the time Angel was done with them, they faced fourth and twenty-two from the nineteen.

I tried *not* to think about Angel during halftime, but my mind wouldn't shut down. Kimi's theory was off base, I was sure of it, and I doubted she believed it anymore. Angel was too sullen, too much of a loner, to be an undercover cop. The police in Federal Way had worked as a team; Angel didn't talk to anyone about anything. He'd eaten lunch back with purple-haired Laurie Walloch and the other druggies on Wednesday, but on both Thursday and Friday he'd taken his tray to different sections of the commons. I had a feeling he wasn't going to sit at the same table two days in a row all year. He was doing everything he could to keep from being noticed by anyone.

But my theory—that he was a cheater—had problems, too. You can't cheat if you don't play, and for the second straight game McNulty was keeping Angel nailed to the bench. Why? Any coach looking for a college job wouldn't sit a stud like Angel without a good reason. So what was the reason?

In the second half, Horst Diamond continued his one-man show. Short passes, long passes, quarterback draws—you name it and he did it. He threw two touchdown passes in the third quarter and rushed for a third touchdown seconds into the fourth. The Roosevelt Roughriders were overmatched, but McNulty showed no mercy, leaving Horst in the game to pad his stats.

The score was 42–0 with just over a minute left when Angel returned. On third down, the Roosevelt quarterback dropped back to pass. Angel, blitzing from the blind side, hit him just as he brought the ball back. The ball skittered on the ground at Angel's feet. He scooped it up, righted himself, and broke into the open field. He was headed to the house; nothing stood between him and the end zone.

Angel should have scored easily, but at the twenty he slowed down, looking over his shoulder. At the ten-yard line he angled toward the sideline, running sideways instead of north-south, almost as if he was waiting for a defender. A Roosevelt wide receiver, the only player closing on him, shoved him out of bounds at the four-yard line.

I looked to the kids seated near me. It was obvious that Angel had been trying *not* to score, but with Lincoln leading 42–0, nobody else was paying attention. Horst came onto the field, took a knee, and the clock wound down to 00:00.

I worked my way down to the field, where I hooked up with Kimi. "We've got to get a story and a photo to Chet by midnight," I said. "There's a byline for us, and money."

"I know. He e-mailed me."

"Should we go to Peet's?"

She frowned. "Couldn't you just transfer my photos to your laptop right now? Then you could pick whichever one fits your story."

"Sure," I said, hiding my disappointment, "that makes sense."

After I downloaded her photos, she hurried off to join Rachel and Marianne. I drove home and forced myself to work. One hundred words aren't very many. I tapped away on my laptop, giving the *who, what, where, when, why,* and *how* of the game. At the tail end I stuck in a sentence about Angel Marichal's fumble recovery. Kimi had a photo of Horst crossing the goal line that fit perfectly. A couple of clicks and I'd e-mailed both the photo and my story to Chet the Jet. I'd have to write a longer version for Alyssa, but that could wait. There wouldn't be another *Lincoln Light* until October.

I woke up early the next morning to look at the *Seattle Times.* Sure enough, there were my one hundred words with Kimi's picture next to them. The article was tucked away in the bottom left-hand corner of the last page of the sports section, but it was there. I read it through, excited and proud to see my name in print. This wasn't the *Lincoln Light;* the *Seattle Times* was a real newspaper with a circulation close to a million. When I reached the end of my story, I stared at the page. Chet the Jet had cut the sentence that mentioned Angel Marichal.

4

DURING THOSE NEXT WEEKS, I spent almost no time with Kimi. We were both covering the football games and the home volleyball games, but she was on the court or on the field, and I was up in the stands. When the games ended, I'd download her photos, go home, write up the game, pick a photo, and e-mail Chet the Jet. I missed the time at Peet's and the excitement of chasing Angel, but mostly I missed being with her.

Lincoln's next four games were against weak teams—Lake Washington, Newport, Juanita, and Franklin. In each game, McNulty gave Angel a couple of series at middle linebacker, and he was on all the special teams. For the Lake Washington and Newport games he wore a new number, sixty-seven, but against Juanita and Franklin he was back to wearing forty-four. He was the only player whose number changed from game to game. No doubt about it—McNulty was trying to hide him.

Trying, but not entirely succeeding. Angel was just too good. On kickoff and punt coverage, he'd break through the opposing wedge as if it were made of sand. The Franklin game was typical. In the fourth quarter, Kenstowicz punted from deep in Lincoln's territory. The Franklin returner, hoping to break a long runback, didn't signal for a fair catch. He hauled the ball in, took one step, and then Angel jolted him with a teeth-rattling tackle that made everyone watching sit up. The ball popped free, and another Lincoln player recovered the fumble. The Franklin kid didn't get up for three minutes, and he never returned to the game. Angel forced fumbles in a couple of the other games, too, and had a couple of interceptions. Lincoln won all four games, pushing their record to 6–0 and moving them into the top ten in the state rankings.

I wrote up every game for the *Seattle Times*. My stories featured Horst, naturally. But when Angel did something great—like jarring the football loose in the Franklin game—I'd include a sentence about him. And every single time, Chet the Jet cut that sentence. The second time it happened, I called and asked him why. "I've been doing this for thirty years," he snapped. "You've been doing it for thirty days. Write your little story, take your fifty bucks, but leave the editing to me." After that I didn't have the guts to complain.

October is when the rain gets serious in Seattle. I knew it would be harder to run after school, but I didn't know how much harder. And not spending much time with Kimi sucked away part of my motivation. I skipped running one Friday, and then both Tuesday and Friday the next week. One day I had a hamburger and fries for lunch; a couple of days later I ate a Snickers. I was losing momentum, and I knew how dangerous that was. Roll a snowball down a steep hill, and it gets fat fast.

5

On the Monday after the Franklin game, Jessica Lathrop stopped me in the hall. Jessica's the best tennis player in the school, and she's the world's most out-front person—no beating around the bush with her, ever. "So you want to go to Columbia?" she said. "I didn't know that."

I looked at her, amazed. I'd told Kimi about Columbia, and I'd told my parents, but no one else. "How do you know about Columbia?"

"I'm a TA in the office. I file stuff for Mrs. Cressy. You had a meeting with your counselor last week. He wrote down your college choices and I filed his notes away. I can't help having eyes. You're not mad, are you?"

"No, I'm just surprised that something that small goes into my file."

"Your whole history goes in there, from preschool on. Some files are an inch thick. But why Columbia, Mitch? I'd be scared to live in New York. Crime and all that."

"Parts of Seattle are pretty tough, too," I said, thinking about the mini-mart. We talked about subways and gangs until the bell rang. I went to English, and as the other kids discussed a short story by Poe, a plan took shape in my mind.

I wasn't cut out for anything dangerous. I'd learned that lesson twice. But you don't have to walk down dark alleys at night or follow troops into battle to be a top-notch reporter. There are war experts who have never heard a single gunshot, who have never even left Washington, D.C. They study history, they pour over statistics, and they end up understanding more than people who are in the war zone. I could be like them. I could investigate Angel Marichal—from a safe distance.

The first thing would be to get a look at his school file. If I could somehow make a copy, I'd get some new facts about him. And those new facts might lead to more new facts. If I found a trail and followed it, I might learn the truth.

In the hall after class, I cornered Jessica Lathrop again, pumping her with questions about the office. Mrs. Cressy was sharp; there'd be no getting files while she was around, but she couldn't be there all the time. "Friday afternoon Cressy leaves early," Jessica told me. Once I'd heard that, my plan came into sharper focus.

That night I called Kimi. We talked about nothing for a few minutes. "I've figured out how we can investigate Angel but not run any risks," I said after a pause.

"How?" she asked, her voice interested yet doubtful.

"If we can get his school records from the office," I said, my words tumbling out fast, "we can find out where he went to school last year, what sports he played, that sort of stuff. Then we can call his old school and talk to people who knew him. If his story matches his records, we stop. If it doesn't, we dig deeper."

"But how can we get his school records?" Kimi said.

"I'm working on a plan. I just want to know if you'd be interested in doing it this way, where we'd do it all on the phone or on the computer."

There was a pause. "It sounds okay, Mitch. Only . . ."

"Only what?"

"If we were caught stealing files, we'd be suspended for sure. My dad would die of shame, and something like that would kill my chances for a top school."

"There'll be no risk for you," I said, thinking fast. "I'm not going to steal his file; I'm just going to make a copy. And I swear to you, Kimi, if I get caught, I'll never tell anyone you were involved."

A long pause followed, and then she spoke. "Before we resort to stealing things, there's something we have to try first."

6

Tuesday I met Kimi outside the commons at the beginning of lunch.

"You ready?" I said.

"I'm ready." She had on a brave face, but she was scared, too.

I pushed the double doors open and we strolled over to where Angel, head down, was eating. "Hey," I said, sticking out my hand and trying to sound breezy. "You're Angel Marichal, right? Special teams star and middle linebacker. I'm Mitch True. This is Kimi Yon. I write sports for the *Lincoln Light,* and Kimi's the photographer. I've got some questions for you, and Kimi wants to take some photos."

I was smiling like a used-car salesman, but Angel stared at my hand as if it were covered in warts. "Leave me alone," he muttered, barely lifting his head.

I sat next to him. "Come on, everybody wants his picture in the paper. There will be another *Lincoln Light* coming out soon. Just a few questions and a few photos and we'll leave you alone." I flipped open my notebook as Kimi took the lens cap off her camera. "Where are you from, anyway?"

Angel put his hand over the camera lens. "No questions, no pictures," he said, and then he picked up his tray and walked over to a table on the other side of the commons, where he sat down, his back to us.

I looked at Kimi.

"We had to try," she said. She paused, and then continued. "Every time I see him, he looks older. No way he's eighteen."

"His file would tell us exactly how old he is, where he went to school last year—all the things we want to know that he won't tell us."

Kimi leaned toward me. "Okay, so explain to me exactly how you think we can get his records."

For the next few minutes, I laid out my plan, step by step. "It sounds like something out of an old movie," Kimi said after I'd finished.

"Maybe," I admitted. "But that doesn't mean it won't work."

She looked down, closed her eyes for a moment, and then looked up. "All right, I'm in." She reached her hand toward me, and we shook. "But there's one more thing. You get caught; I get caught. If this turns out to be a big story, my photos are going to be part of it. I won't take the glory and skip the risk."

7

CHASING ANGEL WAS THE MAIN THING that interested me. I wanted Friday to come as fast as those photons I'd read about in science, but the hours and days plodded on. I had my schoolwork, and Thursday night there was a volleyball game.

I wouldn't have admitted it to Alyssa, but the more sports writing I did, the more I liked it. A sports season has a rhythm to it, and every game is like a new chapter in a book. But unlike a book, there's no flipping ahead to see how it will turn out.

I'd written recaps of all the games, and they were piling up on Alyssa's desk in the newspaper room. However, Danni Shea hadn't finished her interview with our new principal, and the sophomore in charge of Arts and Entertainment hadn't written a word on either the new video competition or the fall play. The newspaper couldn't come out until those articles were completed. Every time I saw Alyssa she'd complain to me: "You're the only one I can count on."

The girls had lost to Inglemoor on Saturday to drop their league record to 8–3. Inglemoor was the defending league champion, so it wasn't a bad loss, but they would have to beat North Shore to get back on track. Contenders or pretenders—Thursday's game would provide the answer.

I found a seat at the top of the gym. Kimi was courtside, camera in hand. As I watched the warm-ups, it all looked familiar. Terri Calvo, Loaloa Toloto, and Chelsea Braker were huddled together. The same was true of Erica Stricker, Rachel Black, and Marianne Flagler. If they hadn't been wearing the same uniforms, you'd have thought they were opponents.

North Shore jumped ahead early in the first game, scoring six straight on a series of spike serves that had the back line totally flustered. The streak of aces started the Lincoln girls sniping at one another, and they kept sniping the rest of the match. The one good thing was that it ended quickly—the trouncing took just over an hour.

I stood and looked over the court for Kimi, thinking she might want to go to Peet's to talk over our plan one last time. I spotted her huddled by the door with Marianne and Rachel, both of whom were near tears. No doubt the three of them would be going off together. I started down out of the bleachers, my eyes on my feet to keep myself from tumbling like Humpty Dumpty.

When I reached the court, I caught Kimi's eye. She gave me a small wave. I waved back and then walked alone into the parking lot. It had been cold and cloudy when the game started; now rain was pouring down. I ran across the parking lot, opened the door, and plopped down in the driver's seat. Before I started the car, my cell phone rang.

"Kimi?" I said, hopeful. "Is that you?"

"Mitch True?" a male voice answered.

"Who is this?"

"Who I am is not important. Just please listen to me. Leave Angel Marichal alone. Don't come to his house. Don't ask questions about him."

My heart raced. "Who is this?" I repeated.

"Angel is one of the good guys. What you're doing can only help the bad guys."

The line went dead. I stared at the phone, hands shaking. Around me, cars inched their way out of the lot.

Finally I started for home, my thoughts churning. The *Times* hadn't mentioned Angel at all, and there'd been only one article in the *Lincoln Light,* but somebody was already warning me off. Angel had a secret, and whatever it was, it was big. The stuff about him being one of the good guys—that didn't fly with me. Good people don't keep things dark. I'd heard that from my dad more than once.

Back in my room, I opened up my American Government book. For thirty minutes I flipped pages, but nothing was processing. Finally I shut the book and flicked off the light.

Who was it that had called? The friend Angel lived with? Had he seen me that night and somehow tracked me down? I didn't like the idea that somebody was out there watching me.

I closed my eyes and tried to sleep, but I couldn't.

Kimi.

Should I tell her about the phone call? The guy hadn't threatened me. All he'd said was to stay away from Angel. Well, that's what we were going to do. We weren't going to talk to him; we weren't going to go to his house. Investigate from a safe distance—that was the plan, and we'd stick to it. The phone call didn't change anything, so Kimi didn't need to know about it.

8

AFTER SCHOOL ON FRIDAY, I met Kimi by the office as planned. We milled around in the hallway for a few minutes. Sure enough, at three o'clock, Mrs. Cressy flung open the main door and strode out, headed toward the parking lot, just as Jessica had predicted. We watched her until she disappeared behind an SUV. Then I opened the office door for Kimi and followed her inside.

I did the talking at the counter. I told Mrs. Scott, the attendance secretary, that I wanted to interview her for the school newspaper. It was ridiculous, since I was the sportswriter, but she didn't know that.

She agreed, so I started asking questions. *What's the hardest part of your day? What do you find most rewarding?* I wanted everything to go fast, but Mrs. Scott talked on and on, telling jokes, and somehow bringing Australia into every other sentence.

Kimi cut her off. "I'd like your picture for the paper."

Mrs. Scott beamed. "Oh, how nice."

This was it.

Kimi snapped a couple of photos, then screwed up her nose. "The light isn't good in here. Let's go out by the flagpole."

Mrs. Scott shook her head. "I can't leave the office unattended. Mrs. Cressy would never allow that."

Kimi smiled. "Mitch can answer the phone."

Mrs. Scott looked me over. I felt as if I had the word *thief* tattooed across my forehead. "Okay," she said, and then she held up a couple of fingers. "Two minutes."

As soon as she and Kimi left, I hurried to the file cabinet marked M-N-O and pulled it open. Quickly I flipped through the *Ms. Madison ... Maguire ... Marino ... Martin.* Where was *Marichal*? It had to be there.

I flipped back. I'd been so nervous, I'd flown right past it the first time. I pulled the file out, closed the cabinet, and hurried to the copy machine.

On the way I peeked out the window. Kimi was snapping photos of Mrs. Scott standing by the flagpole—but they'd be back soon. When I reached the copy machine, I slid the pages into the tray and hit *Start*. A minute later I was shoving the copies into a manila envelope I'd brought along. Two minutes later I had the originals back in the file cabinet. When Kimi and Mrs. Scott returned, I was sitting in a plastic chair across from Mrs. Cressy's desk, paging through an ancient *People* magazine.

Once Kimi and I were clear of the office, I wanted to find some place to look at Angel's records, but Kimi shook her head. "My aunt's visiting," she said as we walked toward the parking lot. "I have to go home."

"You'd rather talk to your aunt than find out about Angel?"

"You don't understand, Mitch. She's not an ordinary relative."

What was that supposed to mean?

I shrugged. "Okay, if your aunt is that important. But when will we look at his records?"

"After tonight's game. You'll write your article and I'll pick out a photo, and then we'll see what we've got. Okay?"

I nodded.

She reached out for the manila envelope. "Let me keep that."

Instinctively, I pulled it away. "Why?"

"Because you'll look, and I want us to go through the file together. We're partners, right?"

She was right—I would go through the papers. I handed the envelope over.

9

I WENT HOME AND READ UP ON INGLEMOOR. They were 4–2 and had a running back who'd been all-league the year before. Their weakness was at quarterback: a freshman who'd thrown a bunch of interceptions and had fumbled the ball away at least once a game.

As I drove to Memorial Stadium, I wondered if McNulty would stop hiding Angel and finally turn him loose. This was the game to do it. Stop the running game and you stopped Inglemoor, because they weren't going to beat you in the air.

Lincoln got the ball first, but went three-and-out because of a personal foul call on a late hit. After Kenstowicz punted the ball away, our defense ran onto the field. I watched closely, wondering if I'd see Angel at middle linebacker right out of the blocks, but McNulty trotted

Clarke out for the first drive. It was a total mismatch—J. D. Dieter, the Inglemoor running back, dominated Clarke. In tight quarters, he ran right over him; in the open field, he had moves that left Clarke tied up. If you never have to throw the ball, what does it matter if your quarterback is shaky?

Dieter sliced through Lincoln's defense, carrying the ball play after play. When he broke a fifteen-yard run down to Lincoln's ten-yard line, McNulty called time-out. I leaned forward. Sure enough, when the team returned to the field, Angel Marichal was at middle linebacker.

I looked around me—no one else seemed to have noticed. I nudged the guy next to me, a kid I knew from calculus named Bill Diggsy. "Angel Marichal's playing. We'll stop them now."

Diggsy grunted. He had no clue who Angel Marichal was.

I guess I'd started thinking Angel was Superman, because I expected him to stop Dieter in his tracks. I'd forgotten that Angel was ice cold and that Dieter was a D-1 scholarship athlete firing on all cylinders. On first down, Dieter took a pitch, raced toward the corner, cut back against the grain, and waltzed into the end zone, untouched. The extra point sailed wide, making it Inglemoor 6, Lincoln 0, with half of the first quarter gone.

There was an uneasy quiet around me. The more people want their team to win, the more pain they feel when their team falls behind.

What surprised me was that I felt it, too.

Once, when my dad and I were talking about college, he told me that I could major in anything I wanted as long as it wasn't philosophy. "What's wrong with philosophy?" I asked.

"The logic part is useless," he said. "People have never been and never will be logical."

I thought about that conversation as both teams took the field for the kickoff. I didn't like Coach McNulty; I didn't like Angel; and I didn't like Horst. The first two were probably cheaters and the third had an ego the size of Mount Rainier. So I should want Lincoln to lose . . . right? When I thought about the team before the game, I always thought of them as *they*. But while the game was going on, when they were right down on the field below and I was surrounded by cheering kids, *they* somehow morphed into *we*.

Blake Stein returned the kick to the thirty-five, and Horst came out throwing, threading the needle with his passes and mixing in a run from Shawn Warner now and then, transforming the silence into cheers. Just when a touchdown seemed inevitable, Horst got clobbered as he let a pass go. The ball wobbled in the air, underthrown by five yards, and an Inglemoor cornerback dived for it, making an incredible interception and killing the drive. Back came our defense with Angel at middle linebacker, and back came J. D. Dieter.

What a battle that was. Dieter was the whole show for Inglemoor, but even though everyone in the stadium knew he was getting the ball on nearly every play, that didn't make him easy to stop. Sometimes he'd break through Angel's tackle and plow forward for seven, eight, nine yards; sometimes Angel would plant his shoulder pads into Dieter's gut and drive him back.

Dieter was too good to be bottled up; Angel was too good to be run over. So throughout the first half Inglemoor picked up a few first downs only to have Lincoln's defense stiffen. Twice Inglemoor got in field-goal range, but both times the kicks sailed wide right. The other drives ended in punts.

Inglemoor's defense wasn't strong, but if you're lucky, you don't have to be good. Throughout the first half, the football gods turned on Horst. The first two drives had ended with a penalty and then an interception; the next two ended with fumbles. And just before halftime, Lenny Westwood dropped a sure touchdown pass. The score at the half remained Inglemoor 6, Lincoln 0.

I don't know what McNulty said to the team in the locker room, but I bet it wasn't pretty, because it was a different Lincoln Mustang team that came out of the locker room.

After a short return of the kickoff, Inglemoor's freshman QB led his team onto the field. Across the line of scrimmage from him, the Lincoln defenders were jumping around, sky-high. Angel was playing middle linebacker; Darren Clarke was on the bench where he belonged.

On first down, the Inglemoor QB handed off to Dieter on what looked like a standard dive play. Angel shed his blocker and was moving in to make the bone-jarring tackle—only Dieter wasn't running. He took one step toward the line of scrimmage, and then turned and lateraled back to the freshman QB. It was the old flea flicker play, and our entire secondary—eager to make the big hit at the line of scrimmage—had dropped coverage. The Inglemoor QB had a weak arm, but his receiver was open by twenty yards. Sometimes when a receiver is completely open, that's the pass that gets dropped, but the Inglemoor receiver looked the ball into his hands and raced seventy-five yards to the house. Inglemoor 13, Lincoln 0. And just like that, Lincoln's momentum was gone.

Still, it was just two touchdowns. I'd seen the Lincoln

offense put up four touchdowns in a half. Only this game Horst couldn't get untracked. He'd get a drive going, and then make a lousy pass, and out would come the punting team. Inglemoor pounded J. D. Dieter at us. He'd manage a couple of first downs on each possession, taking precious minutes off the clock and saddling us with lousy field position. The third quarter ended 13–0, and halfway through the fourth, that same score held.

Then something finally went right. After Angel stopped Dieter on a third and three, the Inglemoor punter shanked his kick. I don't think it went ten yards. Horst came back onto the field with great field position for once, and McNulty went for broke. On first down he sent Lenny Westwood streaking down the center of the field on a post pattern. Westwood soared up between the Inglemoor defenders and somehow pulled the ball down. The two defenders collided, knocking each other off the play. Westwood kept his balance and took the ball to the end zone. Inglemoor 13, Lincoln 7.

After the kickoff, our defense roared onto the field. There was still time; we just had to get the Inglemoor offense off the field. Stop them, score again, and sneak away with a 14–13 win to keep the perfect season alive.

On first down, Inglemoor ran Dieter wide to the right. Our entire defense chased after him. And again the

Inglemoor coach caught us overpursuing, because it was a reverse. Dieter pitched to a wide receiver coming around, and no one was on the opposite side of the field to stop him. The guy ran like a greyhound. The forty . . . the thirty . . . twenty . . . ten . . . five . . . touchdown.

Inglemoor 20, Lincoln 7.

And five minutes later, at the horn, that was the final score.

The undefeated season was gone.

10

THERE WAS AN ACCIDENT in the parking lot, so Kimi and I sat in the dark for half an hour while tow trucks cleared the cars. At Peet's, we got tea and went upstairs. She scrolled through her photographs while I opened my laptop and got to work on my story. Because of the car crash, I had to hustle to meet my deadline.

My headline read LINCOLN FALLS TO INGLEMOOR. I followed that with a brief description of each of Inglemoor's scoring plays, and a line on how Dieter would have run wild had it not been for Angel Marichal and all the tackles he made. I didn't come right out and say that McNulty had been out-coached, but it was there between the lines. When I finished, I downloaded Kimi's photo of the Inglemoor receiver crossing the goal line with the clinching touchdown and e-mailed all of it to Chet the Jet with five minutes to spare.

"Okay then," Kimi said, and I watched as she opened the manila envelope and pulled out the photocopies of Angel's school records.

She turned the pages over one by one, holding them sideways so we could both see. On top was the registration page. After that came a medical insurance form, followed by an emergency contact sheet, neither of which had been filled out. "Flip to the real stuff," I said.

"Let's do this one page at a time. Systematically."

She flipped to the next page—a counselor's notes on a meeting with Angel. *Student missed appointment* was written across the top. "No surprise there," she said. "I sometimes wonder if he's said one word to anybody at school."

"Keep going," I said.

Then came a page recording another missed meeting. And then another. She flipped the page over, and we both froze.

We were looking at a nearly clean sheet of white paper. At the top, in large bold capital letters, were the words *RECORDS REMOVED: BIRTH CERTIFICATE.* Printed underneath was the name Hal McNulty, and beneath was McNulty's signature, along with the date: July 1. I stared at the page, trying to figure out what it meant. "Flip," I said.

Kimi did. Another nearly pure-white page: *RECORDS REMOVED: VACCINATION HISTORY.* Below, again, McNulty's name, printed, signed, and dated. She flipped again: *RECORDS REMOVED: STANDARDIZED TEST SCORES.* She flipped: *RECORDS REMOVED: HIGH SCHOOL REPORT CARDS.* She flipped. *RECORDS REMOVED: MIDDLE SCHOOL REPORT CARDS.* Page after page, all removed by McNulty on July 1.

"That's the last page," Kimi said, looking up. "What's it mean?"

"It means McNulty doesn't want anybody to know anything about Angel Marichal."

Kimi turned back to the top sheet, the registration. She'd gone right past it the first time, but now we both read the page slowly. "Look," she said, tapping the line that read *Expected Date of Graduation.* "January fifteenth."

"He's here for one semester," I said.

She looked up. "This fits with the cheating thing, doesn't it?"

I nodded. "It sure does."

"But it seems so stupid to cheat in high school football. Who cares?"

"McNulty wants to get back into college coaching. He's said that, from the first day he came here. Once Horst graduates, and Warner and Westwood, and the rest of this senior class, the team will nosedive. McNulty has to take the state title this year, or at least make it to the title game. He does that, and he'll get a college offer. Maybe not as a head coach—it's more likely he'd be an assistant. But he can work his way up."

She bit her lip. "If McNulty needs to win so badly, why doesn't he start Angel? Why doesn't he play him constantly?"

"I've thought a lot about that. I think he's playing it smart. If Angel became a big star early in the season, some opposing coach might start asking questions like 'Where did this guy come from?' So McNulty saves Angel for crunch time, sticks him in for the crucial plays, and then gets him off the field before he makes too big of a splash. That's why he has Angel wear different numbers— to throw other coaches off his track."

Kimi looked back toward the papers. "Did you see the date the records were pulled?"

"July first. Why?"

"Remember the first day of practice? That was in mid-August and McNulty acted like he didn't know Angel's name or anything about him. The whole thing was a charade."

We sat, both silently thinking. Finally she looked back at me. "Where does Chet the Jet fit into this? Why does he cut Angel's name out of your stories?"

I told her what Chet had said the one time I'd asked.

"And you haven't asked him since?"

I shook my head.

Kimi frowned, and then she checked her watch. "I've got to get home," she said, gathering up the papers. "Okay if I keep these?"

"Sure."

"One more thing, Mitch. Does the loss to Inglemoor change everything?"

I shrugged. "At first I thought it was a big deal, but the more I think about it, I'm not so sure. The loss will drop Lincoln out of the top ten in the state rankings, and McNulty won't like that. But if they beat Bothell next week, both teams will finish the season 7–1 and in a tie for the league title. If that happens, Lincoln would get the invitation to the state tournament because they'd have won the head-to-head game. That's always the tie-breaker. Once you're in the tournament, rankings don't matter at all."

"I hope they beat Bothell," Kimi said. "If you're right about Angel and we're able to break the story, I want it to be big. Nobody will care if Lincoln is just some team whose season is over."

Early Saturday morning, I checked the online version of the *Times*. My headline was there, and so was every word I'd written about Inglemoor's touchdowns. But there was no photo, and Chet the Jet had cut all mention of Angel.

What was going on? Had the guy who'd told me to keep clear of Angel phoned Chet the Jet, too? That was hard to believe. Chet was a professional writer. Even if the guy had called, Chet wouldn't be scared off by some anonymous phone call. So was it McNulty? He'd told me to feature Horst in every story. Maybe he'd said the same thing to Chet, and maybe Chet was going along, but that was a lot of *maybe*s.

The *Seattle Times* wouldn't run anything I wrote about Angel, but the *Lincoln Light* would. His name ran like a thread through all my stories, but I could do more. The second issue still hadn't been published. I got out my cell and called Alyssa. "How's the paper looking?" I asked.

"Not so good," she said, discouraged. "I wish the other writers were like you. I'm so sick of hearing 'I'll have it for you tomorrow.' We need to get an issue published, and I'm still three stories short."

"Maybe I can help. I've got an idea for a feature on a football player who's new to Lincoln. It won't be too long, and it will fill some space."

"I'd like to say yes, Mitch, but the paper is already top-heavy with your volleyball and football stories."

"Come on, Alyssa. You're the one who said that all kids read is sports. And you want to get an issue out in October, right? This story will be good."

There was a long pause. "Okay, go ahead."

I cut the connection and got to work. Two hours later, I was done.

MAXIMUM IMPACT

Angel Marichal, a transfer to Lincoln High this year, has played a major part in the football team's success despite limited playing time. Marichal's heroics began with the Mater Dei game, where his fourth quarter interception saved the victory that started the Mustangs' season rolling. Marichal continued his contributions with extraordinary special teams in the following games. A one-man wrecking crew on punt and kickoff coverage, Marichal has forced three fumbles, two of which he recovered himself. All three turnovers led to Lincoln touchdowns and played a huge part in the resounding victories. From his middle linebacker position, he has picked off three passes and knocked down at least a half dozen more.

Marichal plays behind Darren Clarke at middle linebacker. However, when the game is on the line, Marichal is on the field. Against Inglemoor, Coach McNulty lifted Clarke and had Marichal play the entire second half. Even though Lincoln lost the game, Marichal's speed and strength held Inglemoor star running back J. D. Dieter in check. In fact, had Marichal played the entire game, many observers believe Lincoln would have won.

Offensive players like QB Horst Diamond garner the headlines in the *Seattle Times*, but ask any coach and he'll tell you that it's defense that wins championships. Marichal's speed and strength make him an intimidating presence. Don't be surprised to see Marichal play more minutes in the future. With Horst Diamond leading an explosive offense and Angel Marichal

spearheading a suffocating defense, this is a team that could still make it all the way to the Tacoma Dome.

When the second *Lincoln Light* finally came out, a spotlight would be shining right on Angel. There'd be no more playing Mr. Anonymous at school, no more hiding in the shadows.

12

ONCE I FINISHED THE ARTICLE, I changed into sweats. For the first time in four days, it wasn't raining. I was about to head out to do my run when Kimi called. "Did you see today's *Times*?" she said. "No Angel."

"I saw it."

We talked in circles for a while, getting nowhere. Finally I mentioned that I was about to go running. "I was, too," Kimi said. "How about we run Green Lake together?"

I agreed, but after I hung up I wasn't so sure. The thought of running the lake with Kimi was scary. Could I keep up? I was running more and walking less all the time, but Green Lake . . .

When I drove up to her house, she came out wearing her John Lennon cap, a white T-shirt, and black shorts. Tucked under her arm was the envelope containing Angel's records.

I drove to the parking lot by the pitch-and-putt golf course. Just as we got out of the car, a couple of the guys from school—Brandon Moyer and Ian Suzuki—came flying around a turn and slowed to a stop, their run over. Both looked from me to Kimi and then back to me again.

We stretched a few minutes before starting. Kimi was light on her feet, almost as if she were gliding. I didn't pound as much as I did when I'd first started running, but I didn't glide.

One lap around Green Lake is about three miles. I counted the yellow stripes that mark off every quarter mile. One ... two ... three ... four—or was that really five? Had I missed one? *Just keep moving,* I told myself.

I could see our starting point, but I wasn't sure I'd make it, when Kimi slowed. "I use the last quarter mile to cool down," she said, lacing her hands together behind her head. "You go ahead."

"No," I said. "I like to cool down, too."

She'd hardly broken a sweat; I was drenched. But I'd done it. In the trunk I had a clean shirt and a towel. I went to the bathroom by the crew house, splashed some water under my armpits, dried myself off, and put the fresh shirt on.

"How about we go to Jamba Juice?" Kimi said when I returned to the car. "We can talk there."

We both ordered raspberry smoothies and carried them to an empty booth. She placed the envelope onto the table between us. "I want to show you something."

She was about to take Angel's records out when I stopped her. I'd been thinking about how Brandon and Ian had looked at her and then at me, as if she were matter and I were antimatter: the slightest touch and the whole universe would explode. "I think I should take it alone from here," I said.

Her eyes flashed. "I thought we were partners."

"We are partners, only . . ."

"Only what?"

"Kimi, if we prove Angel and McNulty are cheating—and I think we will—the entire football season will go up in smoke. You know how excited everyone is. Parents, teachers, and kids—they'll all hate you for blowing the whistle on Angel. They'll say that he was second string, that he didn't play much, that you're just out to make a name for yourself."

"They'll say the same about you."

"I know, but it's different for me."

"How is it different?"

Why was she doing this? Why was she making me say it out loud?

"How is it different?" she repeated.

I took a deep breath and exhaled, trying to phrase it in a way that didn't make me seem pathetic. "Nobody notices me at school. I'm like a piece of furniture—I'm just there. But you're Kimi and . . . well . . . you're wonderful, and everybody thinks you're wonderful. You've got a million friends, but they won't be your friends if your name is connected to this story."

She stared at me, making my face turn red. "You're not just a piece of furniture to me, and I'm not quitting."

"Kimi, I don't think you under—"

She stopped me. "I do understand, and I'm not changing my mind, so there's no point in talking about it anymore."

We sat silently for a moment. Then she spread the papers out on the table. "I went over everything again last night"—her voice was businesslike—"and there's something in here we didn't notice." She pointed to the bottom margin of the registration page. "Look."

I could barely make out some numbers that had been incompletely erased. "What are they?"

"Seven digits—a phone number. My guess is that it's the number of Angel's last school. I bet Mrs. Cressy called about something and then scribbled this number down. I'll look up Houston area codes and call all the possible combinations on Monday. If one of the numbers turns out to be a high school—"

"And I'll go back online again to search for a picture of Angel on the websites of Houston high schools. He's probably using a phony name, which would explain why I didn't find anything on him when I first looked. As good a player as he is, there have to be photographs of him on some website, somewhere."

We talked a little longer, rehashing things we'd said earlier. Finally she gathered the records together and put them back in the envelope. "One last thing," she said. "I understand what McNulty gets by cheating, but what does Angel get? Why would he sneak into some high school two thousand miles from his home just to play football?"

"For the same reason you and I both study hard, why we work on the school newspaper."

"What do you mean?"

"Let's say Angel either flunked out or got kicked out of high school. That means he's fallen off the map as far as college football goes. Without a diploma, he has no chance for a scholarship. But if he graduates from Lincoln and McNulty lands a college coaching job somewhere—even as an assistant—McNulty could bring Angel along with him. A football scholarship to a private school is worth two hundred thousand dollars. If Angel plays well in college, he'll have a chance at the NFL, and those guys make millions. He's got reasons to cheat."

13

I SPENT THAT AFTERNOON helping my dad clean out the shed—we had rats nesting in there once—and then took the stuff we never use to Goodwill. In my room after dinner, I logged on to the Internet and typed *Houston High Schools* into Google. That's when I discovered Houston has over two hundred high schools, counting high schools in suburban districts.

I took out a notebook and got started.

Two hours later I'd made it through nine websites. At the rate I was progressing, I'd need three weeks to finish. That would have been tolerable if I was sure I was eliminating schools, but I wasn't. Two schools had great websites with photos of all the football players—no Angel—so I could cross them off. But the team photos for the other seven were hit and miss: some years were there, some years weren't. I wasn't searching for a needle in a haystack; I was searching for the haystack, too. I put my laptop to sleep, turned the lights off, and lay down on my bed in the dark.

My mind wouldn't turn off, though. In a week the regular season would be over. In a month, the state tournament would be over. After that, it would be Christmas, and pretty soon Angel would be gone, and the story would be gone with him. I got back up, powered up the laptop, and slogged away for another ninety minutes. Then I did sleep . . . hard.

I was dead to the world early Sunday morning when Alyssa called. "Can you help me with the newspaper?" she asked. "I need to finish formatting it and then get it down to the printer this afternoon so the copies can be at school Monday morning. It's three weeks late already."

The more time I spent with Alyssa, the more I liked her. I'd always thought she only cared about makeup, clothes, and who liked whom at school. The newspaper mattered more to her than any of that. As we worked, she'd ask my advice about the order of articles, the size of the headlines, the placement of photos. She didn't take all my suggestions, but she considered them all.

The only argument we had was over the sports pages. I wanted her to run a large photo of Angel Marichal in the top left of the first page with my article on Angel right below it. Alyssa shook her head. "That story goes in the bottom corner with a small photo."

"What's wrong with it?" I asked.

"You know what's wrong with it."

"I don't," I said, feeling the blood rise. "Tell me."

"You should have interviewed him, and you should have included details about his past."

"I tried, but he wouldn't talk to me."

"Okay, fine, I believe you. But that doesn't change the fact that it's skimpy."

She was right—it was skimpy—so I stopped arguing. The photo and article ended up bottom right on page ten, but they were in the paper—and that was what mattered most.

When we finally had the entire newspaper ready, we took the pages to the printer in Pioneer Square. Alyssa wanted him to rush, but he shook his head. "Monday afternoon. No sooner."

Her face fell.

"One more day won't matter," I said. "The important thing is that you got another one out."

I drove her back to Lincoln. "Tell me the truth, Mitch,"

she said as we pulled into the parking lot. "Do you think I'll ever be an editor at a real newspaper?"

I thought for a moment. She wasn't a good writer and never would be, but she had a knack for pulling the best out of people, and she loved the printed word. "Yeah, Alyssa. I do."

We'd worked right through lunch, so when I got home I went to the refrigerator and made myself a ham sandwich and grabbed an apple. I was fine with eating alone, but my mother insisted on sitting with me. "Have you noticed I've been buying lean meats and more fruits and vegetables?" she asked.

My body tensed. "Yeah, I've noticed. And thanks." I took a bite of the apple, hoping she'd let it drop.

"I've thought about why I did what I did, and I'd like to explain."

"It's okay, Mom. Really, it is."

"Dan, I need to tell you this." She paused, and my stomach churned. "Your father and I would have liked two or three children, but things didn't work out for us. For years we tried very hard, and we'd just about given up, and then you came along. You were our unexpected treasure, our miracle. Because of that, I was always afraid that we'd lose you somehow. So from the time you were a baby, I wanted you to be big and healthy. So . . ." She stopped.

"Mom, it's okay. You didn't do anything wrong."

"Yes, I did, but at least now you know why."

14

ALYSSA GOT THE NEWSPAPERS from the printer Monday afternoon. I went back to Lincoln after dinner and helped her stack them up by all the entrances.

Tuesday morning, kids at school had a new *Lincoln Light* in their hands, and most turned straight to the sports pages. I saw them reading my volleyball and football recaps and looking at Kimi's pictures. And every once in a while I'd spot somebody with his eyes on my article about Angel Marichal.

All of it got my adrenaline going, so as I headed into the commons for lunch, I wanted to find Kimi. The moment I opened the door, I heard a loud voice. I looked over and saw Angel, wearing an Iverson Philadelphia 76ers jersey, looming over somebody, his finger jabbing the air, his voice enraged.

I moved toward him, and that's when I realized he was screaming at Kimi. I stopped. She looked impossibly tiny, but she was staring him right in the eye, her jaw set.

The coward in me wanted to drop my head, cover my face, and beat it back out the door. Instead, I stepped forward. "Leave her alone," I said, my voice weirdly high-pitched.

Angel wheeled around. His eyes flashed with recognition. "No, you leave me alone." He looked back to Kimi. "Both of you leave me alone."

"If you mean the article, then—"

I didn't get a chance to finish. He turned back to me, grabbed my shirt at the neck, and pulled me toward him. I could feel a lump in my throat, but I couldn't cry, not with one hundred pairs of eyes on me. "Write about Horst Diamond," he hissed, "or Shawn Warner, or anybody. Just don't write about me. Don't take pictures of me." As he spoke, he kept pulling me closer until I could feel his hot breath on my face. The whole time, I kept my eyes locked on his. If Kimi could stare him down, I could, too. He held me for a long moment, and then he shoved me so hard that I fell back onto the ground and into a chair that clattered across the linoleum floor. For a second I thought he was going to start stomping on me—that's how angry his eyes looked—but instead he walked out.

I got to my feet and slid into the spot at the table next to Kimi. Kids around us were staring, but I didn't care. She was shaking, but she hadn't backed down. My voice had gone squeaky, but I'd stood my ground, too.

The lump in my throat slowly went down, and in its place came a cold fury. *I'm going to get you, Angel Marichal,* I thought. *If it takes me a million hours, I'm going to uncover your dirty little secret, whatever it is. The article today— that was just a taste of what's coming. You'll pay for this.*

We didn't talk during the rest of the lunch period, but when the bell rang, Kimi turned to me. "Thanks, Mitch," she said, and hurried away.

That night after dinner I thought about calling her, but what did I have to say? Better to get on the Web and find something out. I thought God or luck or karma would guide my hand. But ninety minutes and seven Houston high schools later, I still had nothing. My eyes were getting bleary, and I had homework. I logged off.

I saw Kimi before school the next day and told her about my useless night. "You getting anywhere with the phone number?"

"I tried that number with every single Houston area code. Not one was a school. Next I used the number with the nearby suburbs. Nothing." She paused. "The phone number is a dead end. E-mail me the names of some high schools, and I'll start helping you with that."

Every night that week we searched the websites of high schools in Houston—she in her room, me in mine. A couple of times I thought I had him. Antonio Gates at Woodland College High and Pedro Uribe at Austin High both resembled him, if you can look like anybody with a football helmet on. I crosschecked by going back to the schools' webpages. I found a picture of Antonio Gates at the senior prom. He was shorter than Angel, had darker skin, and his ears stuck out. Pedro Uribe was still playing for Austin High.

I didn't ask Kimi how her Internet work was going. If she had anything, she'd tell me. Wednesday leaked into Thursday; Thursday disappeared into Friday. We needed a new idea, or a break, or something. And we needed it soon, because once the season ended, our big story would turn into a little footnote.

15

THAT FRIDAY, Lincoln was playing the Bothell Cougars at Memorial Stadium, with the KingCo 4A title on the line. The winner would advance into the tournament; the loser was done for the year.

With everything in the balance, I was certain McNulty would finally start Angel—and I was wrong. On the opening series Darren Clarke was at middle linebacker, and Bothell went right at him. It was the Mater Dei game all over again. If Clarke played off the line of scrimmage expecting a pass, the Cougars sent their tailback right up the gut for five, six, seven yards. If Clarke crowded the line, the Bothell quarterback would hit the tight end or a slot receiver over the middle in the exact spot Clarke had vacated. They marched right down the field and scored. What sense did it make to cheat . . . and lose? Why have Angel on your team if you're not going to play him?

Lincoln's offense, led by Horst's passing, pushed the ball back down the field. It looked like they'd score and tie up the game, but a fumble after a catch near the twenty killed the drive. As Bothell's offense came back out, I sat forward. *Now!* I thought to myself. *McNulty has to put Angel in now!*

But it was Clarke at middle linebacker, and the Cougars went right back to keying every play call on Clarke's position. Bothell scored a second touchdown on an eight-yard run right up the gut.

Lincoln had to put points on the board to stay in the game. On the second drive Horst remained on target, hitting his receivers in stride, gobbling up chunks of yardage with every play. But on first and goal, the team got hit with an offside penalty, and on the next snap, a holding call. After a couple of botched plays, McNulty sent John Kenstowicz out for the field goal try. Kenstowicz's kick barely crawled over the goal post. Bothell 14, Lincoln 3.

After the kickoff, the Cougars' offense sauntered onto the field—that's how cocky they were. Darren Clarke was in way over his head, but Angel sat alone at the end of the bench, helmet in hand. The third Bothell touchdown came on a feathery touch pass to the tight end.

Things looked terrible, and then they got worse. On the kickoff, Blake Stein had the ball stripped from him. It bounced around for what seemed like forever, but when the whistle blew, a Bothell guy was clutching it to his gut. Two passes and two runs later, the Cougars scored their fourth touchdown. When the first half ended, the score was Bothell 28, Lincoln 3.

As the teams trotted down the tunnel into the locker rooms, the Bothell fans roared their appreciation. And why not? They were two quarters from a trip to the state playoffs. On the Lincoln side, kids and parents sat in stunned silence. It was one thing to lose, but to be annihilated? The season that had begun with the amazing victory over Mater Dei was ending with a pitiful defeat at the hands of Bothell. It was over; everyone knew it.

Everyone except Horst Diamond. Lincoln had the first possession of the second half, and Horst came out red-hot. He'd been on target in the first half, but penalties and drops had killed every drive. Now passes that had slipped off fingertips were hauled in.

Bothell countered by blitzing, but Horst beat that strategy with his scrambling. Most quarterbacks slide to the ground when a safety or linebacker has them in his cross hairs, but Horst enjoyed lowering his shoulder and belting would-be tacklers. His take-no-prisoners attitude was contagious. With each first down, the offense gained confidence. Lincoln marched sixty-five yards in nine plays for a touchdown, scoring when Horst dived over the goal line on a quarterback sneak. Bothell 28, Lincoln 10.

I looked to the sideline. Coach McNulty was clapping his hands, exhorting the team to even greater effort. And then I saw him call Darren Clarke over. He said something, Clarke's shoulders slumped, and then Clarke took his helmet off and headed for the bench. As he was walking away, McNulty looked down the sideline and pointed. Angel Marichal was up an instant later, pulling his helmet over his head, fastening his chin strap.

Angel's impact on the game was immediate. He lined up right behind the nose tackle, crowding the line of scrimmage. On running plays, he charged like a runaway truck, quickly coming up to smash Bothell's running backs into the turf. On passing plays, he was catlike, dropping into coverage and either breaking up passes or slamming receivers to the turf immediately after the catch.

The Cougars managed one first down on that possession before being forced to punt. They got the ball right back when Warner dropped what would have been a first down pass, forcing a Kenstowicz punt. But Angel rose to the challenge again, stuffing the tailback after a two-yard gain, knocking down a pass, and then sacking the quarterback on third and eight. As Horst headed onto the field to take over the offense, he high-fived Angel.

Because they led by eighteen, Bothell's coach figured Horst would be passing on every down trying to score quickly, so they dropped seven guys into coverage. McNulty saw it, and he switched to the running game. Shawn Warner carried the ball five straight times and reeled off at least five yards on every play, breaking the last for a twelve-yard run to Bothell's thirty. The success on the ground forced Bothell to pull the extra defensive backs. McNulty spotted the defensive change and called the perfect play. Horst faked a pitch to Warner, dropped back, and hit Lenny Westwood for a scoring strike.

Bothell 28, Lincoln 17.

That TD knocked the cockiness out of those Bothell guys. Time was on their side—the third quarter was nearly over—but they needed one more touchdown to seal the game, and they needed at least a couple of first downs to change the momentum.

But Angel devastated their line on both first and second down, stopping the tailback both times for no gain. That made it third and ten. The whole stadium was up— the Bothell fans begging for a first down, the Lincoln fans trying to spur the defense to one more great play.

Bothell huddled, then stepped to the line of scrimmage. Angel inched up, ready to blitz. Bothell's quarterback spotted him and changed the play. He took the snap and quickly fired to his tight end over the middle. It was the right call against a middle linebacker blitz—only Angel hadn't blitzed. After his initial step forward, he'd dropped back into coverage. His big hand reached out and tipped the pass. The ball fluttered, far short of the receiver, into the arms of our cornerback. He juggled it for an instant before securing the interception. Four Bothell guys gang-tackled him immediately, but Lincoln had the ball back, deep in the Cougars' territory.

The next drive was like watching a Swiss clock tick off the seconds. Warner sweep right: eight yards. Horst to Westwood on an in route: twelve yards. Warner over right tackle: six yards. Horst on a quarterback draw: seven yards for the touchdown.

Bothell 28, Lincoln 24.

Angel was playing out of his mind on defense; Horst was playing out of his mind on offense. Bothell had no answer for either of them.

And right then, when it seemed certain that Lincoln would pull off the stunning comeback, Bothell started moving the ball again. It made no sense. Angel was still Angel. He was still flying all over the field. So what had changed?

As I watched, I figured it out. Bothell would fake something to the middle, forcing Angel to hold his position for a count, and then they'd run the play away from him. Simple, but effective. Somebody besides Angel was going to have to make a play.

Bothell marched down the field, five yards on one play, six on the next, then another for eight. They were protecting the lead and they were running time off the clock. Six minutes left, then five, then four. Still the Cougars controlled the ball.

Bothell had worked the ball inside the twenty and was facing third and four when McNulty rolled the dice, sending both safeties on a do-or-die blitz. The Cougar quarterback saw them coming, stepped up, avoided the tackle, and slung a bullet to his wide-out, who was running a post pattern over the middle. The guy caught the ball, took two steps, and then was crushed by a savage hit. The ball bounced onto the turf, and a Lincoln player fell on it. The Bothell guy stayed down for a long time, but finally he was helped to his feet and managed to walk off the field on his own. As he did, fans all around the stadium stood and applauded. Then the ref blew his whistle and Lincoln's offense came on the field. Two minutes left. Score a touchdown and they were headed to the playoffs. Anything less and the season was over.

Right when he needed to be at his best, Horst threw his worst pass of the season. The pass hit the Bothell safety right on the numbers—absolutely a cinch interception. Maybe it was too easy; maybe that's why the guy dropped it, or maybe the guy was on defense because he had stone hands. When the ball hit the ground, the safety put his hands to the side of his helmet and dropped to his knees as the groans of the Cougar fans echoed through the stadium.

That was the one bit of luck Horst needed. His next pass was a bullet for a gain of seventeen. After that Horst found Westwood on an out pattern for another nine yards, pushing the ball past midfield. Horst then ran for twenty-two yards on a quarterback draw before he was dragged down. First down—but with only thirty-three seconds on the clock. The Bothell guys were doing everything they could to kill the clock. Would there be time?

The crowd was up as Horst brought the guys to the line. I thought he'd throw the ball to the sideline so the receiver could get out of bounds and stop the clock. Instead, he hit his tight end over the middle for eight yards. Bothell was in no hurry to unpile. Nineteen . . . eighteen . . . seventeen. Horst was jumping around, calling his last time-out, but the ref didn't blow his whistle until the game clock was down to fourteen.

During the time-out, McNulty pulled Horst over to the sideline. He gave him the play, then put his hands on Horst's shoulder pads, and looked him in the eye. I knew what he was saying, even though I was fifty yards away. The ball had to go into the end zone. Anything short and the game clock would tick off the final seconds before there'd be time to run another play.

The ref blew his whistle; Horst trotted back onto the field. The crowd was roaring—Bothell's fans screaming for a stop; Lincoln's begging for a touchdown.

The huddle broke, and now Horst was under center. The ball was snapped. Horst rolled right, toward the wide side of the field, holding the ball as if he might throw, but also as if he might at any second tuck it under his arm and run. The cornerback ran parallel with him, holding back, holding back. Pass or run? Pass or run? Which was it?

Horst seemed to tuck the ball and take off. The cornerback came up to make the tackle, and at that instant Horst stepped back and lobbed a pass over the cornerback's head to Lenny Westwood. Westwood caught it on the three-yard line, turned, and with two steps crossed the goal line. Lincoln 30, Bothell 28. It was the greatest comeback I'd ever seen.

16

AFTER THE GAME, Kimi and I went to Peet's. Neither of us wanted to talk about our investigation of Angel because neither one of us was getting anywhere. I wrote up that football game the way I saw it. INCREDIBLE LINCOLN COMEBACK! was my headline. I started with Bothell's early blitz, and then described the second half defensive charge spearheaded by Angel. Finally I gave Horst props for putting points on the board. I picked two of Kimi's photos to send along—one of Horst and one of Angel. "Chet the Jet has to print what I wrote about Angel," I said to her after I hit *Send*. "There is no way they would have won without him."

But he didn't. The article in the Saturday morning edition of the *Times* included every word I'd written about Horst but not one word about Angel.

I took my normal run—I weighed 176 now—and with every step I grew angrier. In the other games, Angel had only been in for a few key plays. I'd always given Chet the Jet a bit of slack because of that. But this time Angel had dominated the entire second half. To leave his name out of the *Times* was bad journalism.

Back home I made the call before I showered. I didn't want the anger to wash away with my sweat. He picked up on the first ring. "Chet Jetton."

"This is Mitch True."

"Make it quick. I'm busy."

"Okay. I'll make it quick. Why don't you print my articles the way I write them?"

"Why don't I print your articles the way you write them?" he repeated sarcastically. "You're lucky I print anything you write. And those fifty bucks? If it weren't for the photos Kimi takes, you wouldn't get that. Do you even go to the games?"

"Of course I go to the games."

He snorted. "Then what is it with you and this Angel Marichal kid? You got a thing for him? Coach Morris faxes me a stat sheet after each game."

I was totally confused. "What are you talking about?"

"I'm talking about the official statistics of the game. What coaches share with one another and with the press. On the defensive side, it lists things like tackles made, fumbles forced, and interceptions. What you write about

Angel Marichal never jibes with the stat sheet. It's never even close. So that means that at midnight I'm sitting at my computer cutting sentences from your story so that it matches reality."

"My reports are right. It's the stat sheet that's wrong."

"Rob Morris has kept the stats for Coach McNulty for three years, and he's solid. You, on the other hand, are in your first season and have no track record with me."

"But you could call—"

"I have called. I've called McNulty and Morris. They both tell me that Angel Marichal is a decent substitute, but nothing special, and that's why he hasn't started a single game all year. So here's the deal, Mitch. Don't include Angel Marichal in any article you write for the rest of the season. If his name ever shows up prominently on Morris's stat sheet, I'll call Morris and he can fill me in on Marichal's epic achievements. Got it?"

The phone clicked.

I sat, seething. McNulty and Angel were marching side by side to a state title by pulling off a season-long play fake on the coaches and players of the other teams. In January, Angel would be gone from Lincoln. In June, McNulty would follow him. Maybe they'd get away with it; maybe I'd never be able to prove anything. But I was going to keep trying.

17

RIGHT WHEN THE ANGEL INVESTIGATION STALLED, the volleyball team exploded. On Tuesday night I sat in the stands and watched them get trounced by Woodinville. As usual, the two factions on the team spent way too much time arguing with one another and with the refs. But the big story was what happened Wednesday night. The team had spent the night at a hotel in Bellevue. Chelsea Braker brought two bottles of whiskey, and all the seniors got drunk. Terri Calvo passed out in the hotel lobby, and Rachel Black was wandering around in front of the hotel in her nightgown. Six of the girls ended up at the police station.

I heard about all this from Kimi on Thursday before school.

"What were they doing at a hotel in Bellevue?" I asked.

"It was Coach Thomas's idea. After the Woodinville loss, she thought the team needed time together away from the coaches to build spirit. So she rented the hotel rooms for them, and then she left."

"She left?"

"She thought the girls would bond better without any coaches."

"And the hotel was okay with Ms. Thomas leaving?"

"She didn't tell them."

"Wow," I said. "What a story. For sure we can sell this to the *Seattle Times*. We'll scoop Chet the Jet, too. He can't know anything about this." I took a breath. "All right, here's what we do. First, we arrange interviews with the hotel manager and Ms. Thomas and the police. You get photos of the hotel—"

"Mitch," she interrupted. "I'm not taking any photos for this, and I don't want you to write anything."

"You can't be serious. We have to write about this."

"These are my friends. They're humiliated already—don't make it worse."

"Kimi, we have—"

"Just think about it. For one day. How can one day matter?"

My mind was racing, but I forced myself to slow down. "Okay. I'll think about it. For a day."

Back home, I plopped down on the sofa, confused. The stuff with Angel was headed nowhere, but this volleyball disaster was a story. The girls were certain to be suspended from the team and from school. And Ms. Thomas? She'd probably lose her job and might even be banned from teaching. How could I ignore a story that big and call myself a reporter?

I was stretched out, feeling miserable, when my cell phone rang. It was Alyssa. "Forget the volleyball story," she said, as if reading my mind.

"What?"

"None of the girls are eighteen."

"So?"

"They're minors, Mitch. It's against *Lincoln Light* policy to print the names of minors who get arrested. The *Seattle Times* won't run any names either."

"Alyssa, are you just saying this because you're friends with them?"

She snorted. "They're Kimi's friends, not mine. I'd love to run the story. Call Mr. Dewey if you don't believe me."

18

CITY HIGH SCHOOL KIDS basically think suburban high schools are filled with arrogant, spoiled kids who have tons of money. And of the suburban high schools near Seattle, Cascadia—Lincoln's opponent in the district title game—is the most hated. Girls' softball or boys' tennis, the Cascadia Coyotes act as if it is their God-given right to win. Whenever there is some poor sportsmanship—

kids throwing things at the opposing players, parents cursing out refs—Cascadia is involved. Their school colors are silver and black, and their uniforms are identical to those of the Oakland Raiders, which fits perfectly.

The game was at Sammamish Stadium, Cascadia's home field, in the foothills above Bellevue. I didn't bother to ask Kimi if she needed a ride because I knew she'd be going with Marianne and Rachel.

I drove by myself, arriving an hour early. Memorial Stadium, our home field, is a dump, but the Coyotes' stadium is new and plush, like a miniature Qwest Field. The concourses are wide, and they don't smell of pee because homeless people don't live there during the week. Instead of long, hard benches, the seating areas are furnished with contoured seats.

I found a place on the fifty-yard line about fifteen rows up, pleased that my butt slid in without squeezing. When I arrived, a sea of empty seats surrounded me; by game time, the stands were packed. Most of the people around me were Lincoln fans, but Cascadia had so many supporters that they spilled over onto our side, too. Halloween had been earlier in the week, and some of the Cascadia kids were wearing werewolf masks. It was clear they were planning on turning the game into one long party.

I was hoping for a close, back-and-forth game; I was afraid I might see a Cascadia blowout; but I wasn't at all ready for the way the first three quarters actually went down. The game was boring. It was as if both teams had used up all of their energy to reach the district championship and were running on fumes.

Or at least, Cascadia was running on fumes. Lincoln had about one pint of gas. They managed a touchdown in the first quarter, a field goal in the second, and another field goal in the third. Horst didn't make any great passes; Angel didn't play much, and when he was out there, he didn't make any great stops. I felt as though I were watching a practice game in August.

Halfway through the fourth quarter, with the score stuck at 13–0, a Lincoln drive stalled . . . again. Kenstowicz punted and the Cascadia return man caught the ball, took one step, slipped, and went down on his own twenty. The Cascadia fans—or those who were awake—groaned.

I looked up at the clock: four minutes remained. I opened my laptop and starting composing my story for Chet the Jet, trying to think how I could add spice to what had been a bland game.

And that's when everything changed. On first down, the Cascadia QB took the snap and pitched the ball to his tailback. The runner broke left, cut back, and he was clear.

He gained forty-eight yards before he was finally run out of bounds. Cascadia's students and parents—silent for so long—started shouting like madmen. On the very next play, Cascadia ran a pass play off a double reverse. The wide-out was alone on the ten-yard line when he caught the ball, and he walked in for the score.

After the extra point split the uprights, everybody in the stadium knew an onside kick was coming. McNulty had his *hands* team out there—receivers, running backs, even the quarterbacks. The Lincoln guys crowded up, alert. The Cascadia kicker approached the ball. He kicked the top half, and the ball tumbled forward, end over end.

Somebody—I couldn't tell who—came forward to field it, but the ball hit off his shoulder pads. A mad scramble followed, guys digging deep to make the play. There was a huge heap of arms and legs scrabbling for the ball. The refs blew their whistles furiously and started pulling players off the pile. In the stands everyone was silent, expectant. Finally, from the bottom of the pile, a player jumped up holding the ball aloft in triumph and prancing to the sideline like a thoroughbred ready to race.

He was wearing silver and black.

The Cascadia fans exploded. Sure, Lincoln led 13–7, but the Coyotes were in position to steal the game. One more touchdown and Cascadia would be headed to the state semifinal game while Lincoln would be going home.

McNulty didn't mess around with Clarke; he put Angel out there at middle linebacker. And the Coyote coach didn't mess around, either. He went for the knockout on first down. The quarterback lateraled to the halfback on what looked like a sweep play. Instead of trying to make the corner, the tailback drifted back from the line of scrimmage, his eyes downfield. Our cornerback had come up a couple of steps when he'd seen the pitchout, but now he was racing back. The Cascadia receiver was wide open—if the pass had been on the money he'd have scored easily—but halfbacks don't have the arms of quarter-backs. The ball hung in the air just a little; the wide-out had to wait a beat for it to come down, and that extra second gave our cornerback enough time to run him down and tackle him at the eight-yard line.

The Cascadia fans were hopping up and down and hugging one another. I looked up at the clock: three minutes remained. Plenty of time.

On first and goal, Cascadia ran their fullback up the gut for two yards before three guys tackled him. On the next play, the Coyotes' wide receiver ran a fade pattern into the corner of the end zone. It was a timing play, run far away from Angel, but the ball was overthrown. On third down, Cascadia tried a pass to their tailback in the flat. He caught the ball, but Angel and two other guys dropped him in his tracks for no gain.

Fourth down.

Cascadia called time-out. The players huddled around the coach. This was it, their last chance. The ref blew his whistle, and the team huddled at the fifteen. They broke the huddle and trotted to the line of scrimmage.

The quarterback leaned over center, tapped once, and the center snapped the ball. The QB rolled right; Angel streaked toward him on a blitz, but Cascadia had kept the fullback in to help block—Angel wasn't going to get to the quarterback.

I looked to the end zone. Half of Lincoln's defenders were playing zone, but the other half were playing man-to-man, leaving no one in the center of the field. Some-one had blown the coverage. Was it Angel? The center had to be Angel's area. The Coyote tight end moved into the open space.

All the Cascadia QB had to do was lob the ball to him, but the pressure got him. He short-armed his pass, throw-ing it at the tight end's feet. The tight end was a big guy, and he reached down, trying to pick it off his shoe tops. For a moment I thought he had it, but the ball bounced off his fingertips, turning end over end in the air, almost as if in slow motion. The tight end was trying to gain control, but he kept bobbling the ball—and then our safety leveled him, and the football was on the ground, bounding harmlessly away.

Lincoln was headed to the Tacoma Dome, two wins away from being crowned state champion.

The Cascadia fans snarled their way down from the bleachers while the Lincoln fans stayed in their seats to cheer the team. I saw Kimi taking pictures of the players holding up their helmets and saluting the crowd. Horst was in the front, with Warner and Westwood at his side. Angel was far in the back, the only player still wearing his helmet.

The celebration lasted fifteen minutes. After the cheering ended and the players disappeared down the tunnel into the locker room, I walked out into the parking lot. Some drunken Cascadia guys were screaming and swearing as they ran around the parking lot, looking ridiculous yet scary in their Halloween masks. I kept my head down—no way I was making eye contact with any of them.

When I got to the Focus, the man next to me—a guy about my dad's age—had his trunk up and was pulling out his spare tire. "Did they get you?" he asked.

"What?" I said.

He motioned to the cars near us. About half a dozen of them had their trunks up. "Those Cascadia morons slashed a bunch of tires. They got me, and you've got a Lincoln parking sticker in your back window, so I thought they might have gotten you."

I walked behind the car. Sure enough, the back passenger tire was sitting on the rim.

"Flat?" the man called out.

"Yeah."

I opened the trunk, only to discover the spare tire was the wrong size. I carried it over to the man. "This won't work, will it? It looks tiny."

He shook his head. "In the old days, you got a real tire. Today, all they give you are these miserable things." He pointed to the spare tire of his Honda Civic. "Mine's the same. That thing will work. You can limp home with it, but don't try to go on the freeway. Thirty-five miles an hour, maybe forty, tops. Do you know how to change a tire?"

"I've never done it," I admitted, "but I can figure it out."

"I'll help you when I'm done with mine."

The man finished changing his flat just as I got my tire off the wheel. He talked me through the rest. When I finally had the tiny spare mounted, he wished me luck. "Remember—slow."

I eased the Focus out onto the main road and then crawled along in the right lane like a ninety-year-old woman. Sometimes I'd give it a little extra gas, but whenever the speedometer inched much above forty, the Focus shook so wildly that I thought the doors would fall off. It took me nearly twice as long to get home as it had taken me to get to the game.

Up in my room, I whipped out the one hundred words for Chet the Jet in ten minutes. Angel hadn't been the story, so I didn't feel bad about leaving him out. Kimi had e-mailed me a great photo of the dropped pass at the end of the game. Thirty minutes after I'd sat down at the computer, I hit the *Send* button. The next *Lincoln Light* was weeks away, so I could put off my articles for it. I got in bed, flicked off the light, and fell asleep.

THE NEXT MORNING, I had a message from Chet the Jet. *Great article. Didn't change a single word.*

The world is a crazy place. If somebody had told me six months earlier that a professional newspaper reporter would call something I wrote *great,* I'd have sworn that it would be the happiest moment of my life. Now it had happened, and all I felt was depressed.

After I ate a bowl of oatmeal, I drove down to the Ballard Locks to run. I used a bench by the roses to stretch, and then jogged to the fish ladder, up the steep

hill, and across the footbridge toward the Magnolia neighborhood.

When I run, my eyes are open, though I don't really *see*
anything. But that day, as I looked down into the ravine
from the footbridge, I stopped in my tracks. What my eyes
were telling my brain didn't make sense. Half in and half
out of the creek that runs through the steep ravine was a
great blue heron, dead. Somebody had impaled it with
a stick.

I glanced around, uncertain what to do. Finally I started
running again, but I'd only gone a few yards when I pictured the little kids who cross the bridge with their moms
and dads. They'd see what I'd seen.

When I reached the Magnolia side of the bridge, I
slowly worked my way down the slick, steep bank. The
creek below was more like a river, swollen by Seattle's
autumn rains and running fast. I didn't want to lose my
footing.

After about ten minutes, I made it. I inched my way
along the bank of the creek toward the dead bird. Just as
I reached it, another heron came streaking low over the
creek, nearly skimming my head as it swooped, and
landed on a branch nearby.

I was determined to give the dead bird some sort of
burial, but the live heron almost scared me away. I'd seen
herons wading along the shores of Puget Sound. When

they saw something to eat, they hit their prey with the speed of a striking rattlesnake. I'd read somewhere that their beaks were as sharp as ice picks.

Flies swarmed around the spot where the bird had been speared; dragonflies darted back and forth above it. The filmy eyes stared at me accusingly, as if I'd killed it.

It was too gross to touch, so I grabbed the stick and pulled, hoping to yank the bird out of the water. It was much lighter than I expected, and with a few tugs I was able to move it under some nearby blackberry bushes. After that, I laid some fallen Douglas fir branches and some morning glory vines on top of it.

The other heron watched as I covered the dead bird with branches and leaves. It wasn't exactly a proper burial, but it was better than leaving it out in the open. When I was satisfied that no little kid could see the bird from the bridge, I stopped. The live heron eyed me for a long moment, then suddenly flapped his huge wings and flew out of the ravine toward Shilshole Bay. My eyes followed him until he disappeared, and then I slowly worked my way back up to the bridge. I slipped a couple of times, scraping my stomach and arms. For a panicky moment I thought I'd never get back up, but I did.

I cleaned myself off a little and then took my normal run through Magnolia. Instead of thinking about Angel or Kimi, the whole way I kept wondering why anyone would kill such a beautiful bird. Maybe that's why the flash came to me just before I got back to the car. Maybe your best ideas come when you don't try.

It was his clothes: the Eagles cap, the Eagles jersey, and especially the Allen Iverson jersey. That wasn't a Nuggets or a Pistons jersey; it was a Sixers jersey. All the sports stuff Angel wore was Philadelphia stuff. Kimi and I hadn't found a single trace of him in Houston because Angel Marichal was from Philadelphia.

It had been right in front of us the first time we'd seen him.

PART FOUR

I CALLED KIMI as soon as I got home. I told her to try Philadelphia area codes with the phone number and explained why.

After I cut the connection, I paced my room, wondering how many area codes Philadelphia had. It couldn't be that many. And Angel was a city kid—he wouldn't be from some suburb. If I was right, Kimi would be calling back . . . soon. I looked at my watch. How much time had gone by? *Come on,* I thought. *Come on.*

The phone rang. "Aramingo High School in North Philadelphia."

"Did you talk to somebody? What did they say?"

"It's the weekend, Mitch. All I got was voice mail. But it's a high school."

We talked for a few more minutes. She wanted to know what questions I was going to ask when I called Aramingo High on Monday. "I haven't really thought of that," I admitted.

"Well, you'd better start."

I said goodbye, closed my phone, and then just sat, doing nothing. I was on the verge of uncovering a real story—my first real story. I enjoyed the feeling for a full five minutes, and then I got to work. I had to dot all my *i*'s and cross all my *t*'s. Close wasn't good enough; I had to *nail* the story.

First I needed to establish that Angel had been a student at Aramingo High. I used Google to pull up the school's website. I clicked on the demographic tab first, just to get a feel for the place. Right away I could tell Aramingo was tough. The free lunch rate was 90 percent, more than double Lincoln High's. Judging from the number of suspensions, there must have been a fight every day. In my three years at Lincoln I'd never heard of a teacher getting hit by a kid. Fourteen teachers had been assaulted at Aramingo.

I printed the demographic report and then returned to the home page. It took a while, but I finally found a link to athletics. It was hit-and-miss for most sports, but somebody had posted the results of the football games. They were good—7–2 so far this year, 6–3 the year before, 8–2 the year before that. I kept searching for a link to photos, but there were no pictures of players, and there wasn't a roster, either. The football team looked like the best thing about Aramingo, but nobody seemed to care.

I checked the *Philadelphia Inquirer*'s sports pages next. I typed *Angel Marichal* into the search box and got nothing. I double-clicked *Archives,* figuring maybe his history was somewhere hidden in there. A page popped up asking for a credit card number. I leaned back in my chair and stared at the screen. My mother would let me use her card, but I wasn't ready to ask yet. First I needed to talk to somebody at Aramingo High, and I'd have to wait until Monday morning to do that.

The last thing I did was to come up with a phony name for myself. What I did was to take the names of the two Watergate reporters, Bob Woodward and Carl Bernstein, and mix and match. Should I be Carl Woodward or Bob Bernstein? I settled on Bob Bernstein because I figured that under pressure I could remember the double *B*s.

I was just about to call it a night when there was a tap on my door. I went over and opened it up. I expected to see my mom, but my dad was standing there. He had dark circles under his eyes, and his gray hair was uncombed. "Something wrong?" I said.

He shrugged. "That's what I was wondering."

"What do you mean?"

"You don't seem yourself lately, Dan. You seem . . . I don't know . . . tense. It's been a long time since you've come in and watched a game with me, and at dinner you're awfully quiet. No jokes, no funny stories about school." He paused. "Anything you want to talk about?"

"Everything's fine, Dad. I've just been really busy."

He nodded. "Okay, but if you ever need to talk, I'm here. Remember that."

I watched him head downstairs, and it struck me that just as I'd been getting older, he'd been getting older too, and so had my mom.

2

I FIGURED SCHOOL STARTED around eight in Philadelphia, which would be five a.m. in Seattle. The first hour or so the office at every high school is swamped, so I decided not to call Aramingo High until nine thirty their time.

I watched the minutes tick off, one by one. Finally I keyed in the number. A guy answered on the first ring, but not an adult. "Aramingo High School," he muttered, the words slurring together.

I put on my most adult voice. "This is Bob Bernstein. I work on the sports desk of the *Seattle Times* in Seattle, Washington. We've got a football player out here who transferred from Aramingo to one of our schools. He's having a good year, and we're considering doing a feature story about him. Could you put me in touch with your football coach or assistant coach? I'd like to get some background information."

"The football coaches don't work here," he said. "They just coach."

"How about a phone number?"

"You kidding? We don't give out phone numbers. What's the guy's name? If he played on the football team, I can tell you about him."

"I'd prefer to talk to the coach," I said.

His voice grew sharp. "You want help or not?"

"Okay," I said, my mouth dry. "He would have played for Aramingo last year or maybe even a few years ago."

"What's the guy's name?"

I swallowed. "Angel Marichal."

"No Angel Marichal ever played here."

My heart sank. "You sure? How about just Angel? Maybe his parents divorced and he changed his name."

For a long time there was nothing but silence. I could feel the guy thinking. "What's he look like?"

His voice had changed from hostile to interested. It was as if we'd switched roles, and now he was pumping me for information.

"Mexican guy. Dark hair, dark eyes. Six three, over two

hundred pounds. Strong and fast. Great arm. Quick feet. Hard tackler."

"Position?"

"He's playing middle linebacker," I said, choosing my words carefully, "but that's because his team's got a helluva quarterback. My guess is he might have played quarterback at Aramingo."

"You sure he's not Puerto Rican? We had a Puerto Rican guy play quarterback a few years ago."

"I don't know. I guess he could be Puerto Rican."

"What's your number? I know somebody who's going to want to talk to you."

"Is this a coach who's going to call me?"

"Just give me your number."

"It's 206-879-3078. It's a cell phone."

"And your name again?"

I flushed. "Bob Bernstein," I said, thankful I'd settled on the double *B*s. As soon as the words were out of my mouth, the phone went dead.

3

THE GUY AT THE OTHER END wasn't interested in Angel's football career at Aramingo, and he didn't care about

Angel's football career in Seattle. Something else was going on. But what?

The best thing was to take my time. I'd been on Angel's trail since August; I could give myself a few hours more. I turned my cell off. When the guy from Philly called—and I knew he'd call—his number would show up on my cell. I'd call him back when I was ready to talk to him, and not before.

I saw Kimi at lunch.

"So?" she said, her voice an excited whisper. "Tell me."

I described the phone conversation with the person at Aramingo.

"What do you mean it wasn't about football?" she asked.

"You can tell when someone is talking sports. This guy wasn't."

She looked at me, skeptical.

"You can," I insisted.

"Okay, then what was he talking?" she asked.

I didn't have an answer.

All day I fought the temptation to turn on my cell. When school ended, I did my normal run through a light rain. I now weighed 170 for the first time since I'd been a sophomore. I returned home, took a shower, and only then turned on the cell.

Two New Voice Messages, the screen read. I scrolled to the call log. Two messages, but there'd been four calls—every two hours, like clockwork, and all from the same number. This guy really wanted to talk.

I sat for a moment, preparing myself. The person at the other end didn't have to know what I suspected. I'd ask him about guys on the team two or three years ago. I'd pretend to be only mildly interested. Later, if I had to, I'd tell him more.

I took a deep breath and hit the call button.

One ring. Two rings. A third. Then a voice: "Yeah."

"This is Bob Bernstein in Seattle. I called Aramingo High—"

"Yeah, yeah," he interrupted. "I know. I know." He paused. "This guy. This Angel guy. You fax me his photo and I'll tell you if he's from here. You got a fax machine, right?"

This wasn't what I'd planned on, but it made sense. What was the point of talking if it was the wrong guy? "Yeah, I've got a fax machine."

"All right. Here's the number." He rattled off ten digits, and I had him repeat them.

"And what's your name?" I asked.

"You don't care what my name is. This is about Angel."

"I do care what your name is."

He snorted. "Okay. My name is Juan Doe." A second later the phone went dead. Everything about the guy felt wrong, but he was my only contact.

My parents were still at work, but I knew they wouldn't mind if I used the fax. I went down to the little study off the TV room, laid Kimi's photo of Angel on the tray, and punched in the numbers the guy had given me. The machine sucked in Angel's face, whirred awhile, went silent, then spit him back out.

I'd barely made it back to my bedroom when my cell rang. "Where's he live?" the voice demanded.

"What?"

"Angel. Where's he live?"

"Hold on," I said, trying to put some steel into my own voice. "I'm the one asking the questions."

Silence.

"All right. How about we trade information? You tell me something I want to know; I tell you something you want to know. Fair?"

I didn't like it, but I didn't have a choice. "Okay."

"So," the voice said, "where's he live?"

"Seattle."

"Don't play with me. That's no good. I want a street and a number. We've got some homeboys out there who are going to pay him a visit, once you give me the address."

I thought of Angel's little house at 2120 Elmore, but I didn't say the address out loud—not to this guy. "There are probably a thousand kids playing football in Seattle," I said. "I don't know the home address of a single one. I'm a reporter, not the mailman. Now, how about you tell me about his time at Aramingo?"

"Hey, Mr. Reporter. You give me an address and I'll give you some information, including his real name."

"I told you: I don't know his address."

"Call me back when you've got it, and we'll do business."

4

I CLOSED UP THE CELL and tried to picture the guy at the other end. I didn't like the image that came up. There was something wrong about his voice. One thing was for sure—I didn't want to talk to him again. And maybe I wouldn't have to.

I had the name of Angel's school. I had a good idea of the years he played and his position, and I knew he had changed his name. Aramingo High had a terrible website, but that didn't mean there wouldn't be a record of his games on other websites. The place to look was the archives of the *Philadelphia Inquirer,* which meant I'd need a credit card.

I could call my mom at work, get the number, and start, but it didn't seem right to do it alone. Kimi had started us down this path; she should be with me as we neared the end.

I called her cell, but after one ring was transferred to voice mail. She'd mentioned her battery wasn't holding its charge, so I tried her home phone. Her father picked up. "You a boyfriend?"

"No. I'm Mitch. I work with her on the newspaper. You've met me. Can I talk to her?"

"You the fat boy?"

I winced. "Yeah."

"She not home. I tell her you call, Mitch."

"Do you know when she'll get home?"

"Goodbye, Mitch." The phone clicked.

I lay down on my bed, closed my eyes, and started to think about just how big a bombshell I was about to explode. If everything broke right, Lincoln would win the semifinal game, and during that time, Kimi and I would nail down the story, making everything airtight. And then, right before the title game, we'd publish.

If all those pieces fell into place, Angel Marichal—or whatever his name was—would be declared ineligible.

Lincoln High would forfeit all its victories. Coach McNulty would be fired. For the first time in the history of Washington, the state championship game would be canceled. A story like that would make ESPN's *Sportscenter.* I was imagining myself being interviewed when my cell rang. "What is it, Mitch?"

I explained.

"I can't go out tonight. My aunt's here. You go ahead and print whatever you find on the *Inquirer's* website. You can tell me what you find."

I felt my body sag. The aunt again. I wanted us to make the discovery together. "How about tomorrow night? Could you come then?"

5

THE NEXT NIGHT AT DINNER I told my parents that Kimi was coming over to work on a newspaper article. As soon as I finished my explanation, my mom gave me a *you've-finally-got-a-girlfriend* smile.

"It's an article for the newspaper," I repeated. "That's all. I'm going to need to use your credit card to access some archives."

"How much?" my father muttered.

"Around twenty dollars. I'll pay you back."

"If it has to do with school, we pay," my father said.

Kimi was waiting on her porch at seven. When we pulled up in my driveway, Mrs. Marilley, our next-door neighbor, was getting into her car. Mrs. Marilley isn't exactly my father's favorite neighbor. She works the night shift at Safeway, and when she gets home, she lets her hound out. "Big Red loves to run in the moonlight" is what she says. "Big Red loves to poop on our lawn" is what my dad says. Normally Mrs. Marilley pays no attention to me, but now she was waving, the whole time sneaking peeks at Kimi. I could see her mind working: *"I wonder what that pretty Asian girl sees in him."*

When I opened the door to my house, I expected to see my mom sitting on the sofa, eager to meet Kimi, but the living room was empty. Instantly I knew that had been my dad's doing. I was going to have to find time to watch a game with him again, soon.

I had cleaned my room and pushed two chairs up to the desk. We sat side by side as I logged onto the *Philadelphia Inquirer*'s archive page. The fee was $21.95 for the right to print twenty articles. I entered the credit card information and looked at her. This was it.

We tried different search combinations. *Angel + high school football + quarterback.* The results were weird on that one—2,754 articles, the fourth of which was about some Penn State quarterback who met Hillary Clinton in Indiana, and the sixth one about the Los Angeles Angels.

"Add the years you think he played and put in the word *Philadelphia*," Kimi suggested.

I did it—1012 articles, but at least most of the hits concerned sports.

"Leave out *Angel*," Kimi suggested next, "and put *Aramingo High School* in its place."

I typed, hovered my finger over the *Return* button, and then tapped.

Eighty-four hits, and the entire first screen was about Aramingo High football. "If there's anything, it's here," I said.

"Can you search inside these articles?" Kimi asked.

I opened a drop-down menu. "Yeah."

"Okay, now add *Angel*."

I did it, then hit *Return*.

Sixteen hits over four years.

"Click on the oldest one," Kimi said.

A picture came up first. The name below it was Angel Delarosa, but it was Angel Marichal. A younger Angel Marichal, an Angel Marichal with brighter eyes, but Angel Marichal. The headline read ARAMINGO HIGH RESTS HOPES ON TALENTED FRESHMAN QB.

Kimi looked at me, and then wrapped her hands around the back of my head, pulled me forward, and kissed me on the forehead. "We did it, Mitch. We did it."

I printed all sixteen articles, and for the next ninety minutes we flipped through them, helter-skelter, taking turns reading aloud every paragraph that mentioned Angel, both of us too excited to do anything systematically. Then, suddenly, Kimi stopped. "Oh my God," she said, looking at her watch. "I have to go home. I haven't done my calculus homework."

In the car, neither of us spoke. As we drove along, the strange phone call I'd gotten after the volleyball game came back to me. *Angel is one of the good guys.* Why would the guy say that? What could he have meant? I wanted to tell Kimi about the phone call and ask her what she thought, but she'd ask why I'd kept the call secret, and how would I answer her?

When I pulled up in front of her house, Kimi didn't get out. Instead, she looked out the window, away from me. "Somehow I feel sorry for Angel," she said. "Our story is going to make things tough for him."

I was fighting the same feeling. The Angel in the *Inquirer* photographs had looked so young, so eager. "The guys we should feel sorry for are his teammates," I said, talking to myself as much as to her. "Because Angel and

199

McNulty cheated, their season is going to blow up. And how about the players on the other teams, the guys that Angel dominated? They shouldn't have had to play against a grown man. That wasn't fair."

She looked back at me. "You're right, Mitch. But his eyes—he just seems so sad."

After she went into her house, I drove home. I made myself a cup of tea—I'd actually started to like tea—and carried it upstairs. I sat down at my desk and suddenly felt overwhelmed. I had to write a term paper for my government class and an essay on modern American poetry for English. I had calculus homework every night, and two physics labs due right after Thanksgiving. And there, on the floor, were sixteen articles about Angel, sixteen articles that I had to turn into a story that would destroy Coach McNulty's career, end the football team's dream run, and make me the most hated person at Lincoln High. I didn't know where to start, so I finished my tea and went to bed.

6

THE NEXT DAY WAS STRANGE. Kimi and I were on the verge of turning the school upside down, but no one else had a clue. It was like knowing about an earthquake before it was going to hit.

Once the school day ended, I made my way down to Gilman Field to watch football practice, something I hadn't done in a long time. Coach McNulty was going easy on the guys. They had their helmets on, but there were no pads and no hitting. It made sense—after months of smashing into one another and players on other teams, the guys must have been sore to the bone.

My eyes were drawn to the second and third stringers, the guys whose names and pictures were never in the paper. They weren't getting scholarships anywhere; they played because they loved the game. I wasn't the one taking the season from them. It was Angel who'd cheated, McNulty who'd let him cheat—but I still felt guilty.

When I left the practice field, it was too late to run. I ate dinner, climbed upstairs, and did the calculus I absolutely had to complete that night. It had started to rain during dinner, and now the rain was pelting my window. I finished the calculus and then stared at the file holding the sixteen articles about Angel. For months I'd been searching for clues to Angel's past, but now I wished the whole thing would go away. Is that how all reporters felt, I wondered, when they were on the verge of nailing a story? Did they all feel sick at heart about what the story might do? Still, if I was going to be a reporter, I had to let the chips fall where they would.

I opened the file and got started.

There was still one way that Angel—and Coach McNulty—could be in the clear. If Angel had been injured early in one of his seasons at Aramingo High, there was a chance he might have been given an extra year of eligibility.

The odds were one hundred to one against it. If Angel was eligible, why would he have changed his name? Why would McNulty have hidden him? Why would his school records be locked up in McNulty's office? One hundred to one? The odds were more like one thousand to one against it. But I had to check it out.

From the upstairs closet I pulled out a roll of Christmas wrapping paper. I brought it to my room, cut off a six-foot section, and flipped it over to the white side.

For the next three hours, I made a timeline of Angel's career at Aramingo, compiling as thorough a record as I could—freshman year to senior year.

I finished around midnight. Angel had played about half the time as a freshman, was the starting quarterback as a sophomore, and was all-city by the end of his junior year. There was one odd thing—for the first five games of his senior year, his name was all over the sports page.

Aramingo High was undefeated, and then—right in the middle of the season—he disappeared.

I'd have liked to know what happened, but it didn't really matter. A guy plays five games and then blows out his knee, it's his tough luck. No conference is giving a player a year of eligibility back once he's played half a season.

Besides, there was nothing in the newspaper about an injury, which meant it was probably something else. Maybe he failed his midterms, or got suspended from school for fighting or drinking or drugs. He wouldn't have been the first player to screw up.

I pinned the timeline to the wall and stared at it. Numbers don't lie. I had the dates, the games, the touchdown passes, the wins, the losses. And pictures don't lie, either. I had photos proving that Angel Delarosa and Angel Marichal were one and the same. Angel hadn't been eligible to play one down in Seattle, and he'd been in every single game. I had him, and I had Coach McNulty. I had them cold.

I wrote the story the next night. I started right after dinner and finished around eight thirty. The timeline made it simple. When the facts are right, you lay them out and they speak for themselves. Once I finished, I called Kimi. "You got your photos?"

"I got them. Let's go to Peet's. I can read your story and then pick the photos that will work with it."

We sat at our usual counter upstairs, and I thought about how much I liked being with her. She read my article while I flipped through all her photos of Angel.

"It's great," she said, looking at me when she finished. "It is so clear and convincing." I felt a surge of pride. "So what photos should we use?"

"I think these," I said, pointing to ones she'd taken in the cafeteria.

She looked disappointed. "Really? They're so plain."

I had downloaded and printed a photo of Angel during his junior year from the *Philadelphia Inquirer*. I laid the Philly photo next to hers. Angel looked younger in the Philly photo, but there was no doubt it was the same guy. "Plain is better. The *Times* could print them like this. See?"

"Yeah, yeah," she said, her head nodding up and down. "You know, Mitch, there's one last thing we have to do before we bring the story to the *Times*."

"What's that?"

"Show the article to Mr. McNulty and to Angel."

It was like getting a cup of ice water in the face. "Are you crazy? McNulty will go berserk. So will Angel. Remember how he acted the last time?"

"They've got to have a chance to give their side."

"They don't have a side, Kimi. It's all there in black and white."

"Mitch, what would a real reporter do?"

That stopped me. "You're right," I said after a long moment. "And I need to call Philadelphia again, too."

It was her turn to be surprised. "Why Philadelphia?"

"Angel played five games as a senior, and then he disappeared. No mention of any injury, so probably he got kicked off for drugs or drinking or grades. But a newspaper can't publish *probably*. Readers want to know what happened."

Once we'd finished our tea, I drove Kimi home and returned to my own house. I went upstairs, flicked on the light, opened my laptop, logged into my e-mail account, and clicked McNulty's e-mail address in my list of contacts. *We need to talk about Angel Marichal,* I wrote. *I've written a story about his past you will want to read. M. True.* I paused one second, then hit the *Send* button.

7

THE NEXT MORNING I checked my laptop to see if McNulty had replied to my e-mail. Nothing. Philadelphia was next on the list.

I had the number of the guy I'd sent the fax to in my call log, the guy who'd called himself Juan Doe. I scrolled to it and hit the green button. The phone rang a couple of times. "Yeah," a voice said.

"Hello, I'm Bob Bernstein," I said, "calling from—"

"How come you didn't call back?" the voice interrupted, angry.

"I'm calling now," I said, keeping cool.

"So where does he live?"

I gave my best attempt at an unconcerned laugh. "I told you: I don't know. Listen, I'm calling because I'm confused. Angel seemed to be having a good final year at Aramingo High, and then he just disappeared. What happened?"

"You don't know what happened?"

"No, I don't."

There was a pause. "You give me his address, and I'll tell you all about what happened."

"I don't know his address, and there's no way I can get it. He's not in the phone book."

"But you know his school. So you tell me his school."

"If I tell you his school, you'll tell me why he didn't play out his senior year."

"That's the deal."

"All right. He goes to Lincoln High School."

"And that's in Seattle? Right in the city?"

"Yeah, in Seattle. Abraham Lincoln High School. It's in the Ballard neighborhood. So now you—"

The phone clicked.

I stared at it, angry. What was the deal with this guy? I was done calling Philadelphia. I opened my computer and checked my e-mail. Still nothing from McNulty. I was trying to be a responsible journalist, but what can you do if people won't talk to you, won't read your e-mails?

I've got an iPod Touch, and in my morning classes I used it to sneak peeks at my e-mail. Nothing, nothing, and more nothing. In the hall after lunch, I spotted McNulty. I looked him square in the eye, but he looked right through me.

After school Kimi was waiting for me at my locker. "So, what did the guy at Aramingo say?"

"He hung up on me."

"How about McNulty?"

"I e-mailed him, but either he hasn't read it or he deleted it without opening it."

She stood still, thinking. "Then we have to confront him face-to-face. We can talk to him before he goes to football practice." With that, she headed toward the gym. I grabbed my coat out of my locker, slammed it shut, and hustled to catch up.

McNulty was coming out of his office just as we reached the gym. Kimi looked to me. "Coach," I said, my voice loud, "did you read my e-mail?"

He didn't even stop. "No, I didn't read your e-mail. I've got a state semifinal game to coach this weekend, in case you've forgotten."

He strode down the hall toward the doors leading to the parking lot. The players were piling onto the bus that would lead them to Gilman Field for practice. Kimi and I stood watching, too bewildered to move. When McNulty opened the building door and stepped outside, I broke into a run. I caught up with him as he was stepping onto the bus. "I know about Angel and Philadelphia," I shouted, and his head jerked around. "Aramingo High. I've talked to people there. You won't get away with it."

The color drained out of his face and his mouth dropped open. He looked as if he was about to say something, but before he could speak, the bus doors hissed shut. "Read my e-mail," I shouted as the bus lurched forward.

8

SATURDAY'S SEMIFINAL GAME was in the Tacoma Dome, an hour from Seattle. Kimi went with Marianne and

Rachel, which was okay by me. I didn't mind having some time alone. Once I hit the freeway, I turned on the CD player and listened to the Beach Boys, loud. Those guys had it easy. Surfing and cruising and making out with girls—living back then must have been like not having a brain.

I pulled off the freeway into the parking lot, showed the usher my press pass, and found an end zone seat away from most of the Lincoln kids, but still close to the field.

Lincoln's semifinal opponent was Lakes High, a school near Tacoma. They looked great through warm-ups—big, strong, and fast. But then, there were only four teams left in the tournament. All of them were big, strong, and fast.

After watching the Lakes Lancers for ten minutes or so, I turned my eyes to Lincoln. As usual, the team was warming up in small groups spread out from the fifty to the end zone. It was like every other warm-up before every other game except for one thing—I couldn't find either McNulty or Angel.

My cell phone rang. Kimi. "Did you see Angel and Mr. McNulty?" she said.

"No. What happened?"

"They were arguing with each other. Really arguing. At one point, Angel got right up into McNulty's face."

"What were they saying?"

"McNulty's voice was low. But I heard Angel. He said that he didn't care if it was dangerous, that he wasn't running away again."

"Where are they now?"

"They're coming out of the tunnel. Angel's got his helmet on, so I guess he's playing." She paused. "Mitch, what's going on? Running away from what? And how could it be dangerous? Did we miss something?"

The public address announcer told everyone to rise for the national anthem. "I don't know, Kimi."

I closed my phone and stood. After the anthem, the captains strode to midfield for the coin toss. Angel was off by himself, but instead of having his head down, his eyes were scanning the stands.

Lincoln had the first possession and promptly moved the ball downfield. Around me Lincoln kids were cheering loudly, but I was only half there. I knew Horst was on target with his passes, and I knew Shawn Warner was running strong, too. I even took notes. But as play followed play, Kimi's question—*Did we miss something?*—kept gnawing at me.

My eyes went back to the field just in time to see one of our wide-outs drop a third-down pass inside the ten-yard line. Lincoln's fans groaned, but a minute later were cheering when Kenstowicz, steady with his kicking all year, split the uprights from twenty-eight yards away. Lincoln 3, Lakes 0. The drive had taken six minutes.

Lakes's receiver took the kickoff out to the thirty before he was tackled. The defense trotted onto the field. I sat up, and there he was, Angel Marichal, trailing the other guys, but on the field.

For the first time he was a starter, and for the first time he wasn't right. He kept sneaking peeks into the stands, scanning every section, just as he'd done when he'd stood along the sideline. Who was he looking for?

Lakes's star was Gene Wang, a running back with power but not much speed. He was a north-south runner—nothing fancy, just good old smash-mouth football—three yards and a cloud of dust. Lakes strung together first down after first down until they were inside the ten. Facing third and goal from the six, the quarterback handed off to Wang on a draw. Wang put his shoulder down and drove right into Angel, bulling through the tackle and into the end zone.

Lakes 7, Lincoln 3.

All year the center part of the field had been off-limits whenever Angel had been playing at middle linebacker. His focus had been 100 percent. But now his head was on a swivel, looking this way between every play. And so was mine. My eyes kept going around and around the stadium, trying to figure out what was going on.

Football is intense. If your mind isn't in the game, your body's going to take a beating. And that's what happened to Angel. Lakes took the attack right up the gut, knocking him back, pushing him around, and eating up the clock.

They did everything right except put up points. That was because of John Kenstowicz. Horst wasn't getting much going against the Lakes defense, but Kenstowicz was having the punting game of his life, booming one high spiral after another, and our special teams were special, pinning Lakes deep in their own territory after every one of Kenstowicz's punts.

Force a team without speed to go eighty or ninety yards, make them use a dozen plays, and chances are something will go wrong. On one drive the Lakes quarterback botched a handoff to Wang in the red zone. The ball rolled along the line of scrimmage until one of our linemen fell on it. On another, a Lakes receiver had a pass hit him in the chest and carom to a Lincoln cornerback for a drive-killing interception. Lakes totally dominated the game, but when the clock ran to 00:00 ending the second quarter, their lead was just 7–3.

9

I WATCHED ANGEL as he ran off the field at halftime. The rest of the guys on both teams ran with their heads facing forward, but his eyes were still searching the stands. He couldn't play if his mind was somewhere else, which meant Lincoln couldn't win. At least that's how I saw it.

When the teams returned for the second half, Coach McNulty pulled Angel to the side. There was no yelling, no argument. Even from far away I could tell that. McNulty put his hands on Angel's shoulder pads and looked straight into his eyes as he spoke. There was something almost gentle about McNulty, a word I never thought I'd use to describe him.

Whatever McNulty said worked, because during that first defensive series Angel looked like Angel. On first and second down, he clogged the middle, assisting on two tackles. On third and six, he destroyed the blocking scheme on a screen pass, dropping Wang for no gain.

Once Angel focused on the game, I did the same. I'd almost nailed the big story, the story of Angel cheating. In the meantime, I had the small stories to write, too. Chet the Jet was up in the press box, so I wouldn't be writing a recap for the *Seattle Times*. But another *Lincoln Light* would be coming out before the Christmas break. My article on this game and the next—if there was a next— would be read by every student and teacher in the school, and most parents. I blocked out all of Kimi's questions and concentrated on the game.

Neither team scored in the third quarter, but that doesn't mean nothing happened. The offenses struggled, not because they were bad, but because the defenses were good. Some of the hits were so hard, I could hear them way up where I was sitting. Three guys—two from Lakes and one from Lincoln—had to be helped off the field. My bet was that all three had concussions.

The defenses were so fierce, it seemed impossible that either team would ever score. Then, midway through the fourth, Lakes caught a break. Lincoln had the ball, third and one, near midfield. Warner took the handoff and plunged into the line. The Lakes defensive line stopped him cold, but Warner slipped to the left, legs driving, giving everything he had to get that first down. A Lakes safety smacked down on the ball with his fist and it popped loose. Somebody kicked it, and a Lakes lineman had it jump right into his hands. He rumbled downfield for forty yards before he was tackled from behind at the Lincoln twelve-yard line.

The Tacoma Dome exploded. Lakes fans roared for the clinching touchdown; Lincoln fans exhorted their defense to hold. Lakes sent Wang off left tackle for three, then off right tackle for three more. On third and four, the quarterback faked to Wang and then ran a bootleg right that nearly fooled Angel. When they unpiled and measured, Lakes was inches short.

Fourth down.

The Lakes fans were up screaming: *"Go! Go! Go!"*

The Lakes coach sent in two tight ends. Lincoln's linemen dug deep, the linebackers filled the gaps. Just before the snap, Angel shot his gap, his timing perfect. As Wang took the handoff, Angel drove into him, knocking him back for a loss of two. Angel raised his hands as he raced off the field, followed by the rest of the defense, all of them jumping and hitting one another out of sheer joy.

It was an incredible goal-line stand, but it wouldn't mean a thing unless the offense could score. Under the shadow of his own goal line, Horst looked over his shoulder to make sure Warner was positioned correctly. He took the snap, turned, and a second later Warner hit off right tackle where he was stopped after a two-yard gain. Or at least that's what I thought.

And it was what Lakes's defense thought, too.

But Horst hadn't handed off. He had the ball on his hip, and he had Coby Eliot running down the sideline five yards clear of any defender.

Horst laid the pass out into the center of the field, a long, high, gorgeous spiral. Eliot had to slow just a bit to take the ball in, and that's what kept him from racing untouched to the end zone, but the play still gained over sixty yards.

The Lakes guys were stunned; Horst hurried his team to the line before they could recover. He ran the next play without a huddle, a simple pitch to Warner. Lincoln had run a similar play earlier and had gained next to nothing, but this time Warner cut back and bulled his way down to the fifteen before he was finally brought down.

Two plays and nearly eighty yards. Again Horst hustled the team to the line, where he again went with a quick snap. He dropped back, looked to pass, and then tucked the ball under his arm and took off on a delayed quarter-back draw. The Lakes guys were so confused that only the outside linebacker knew what was happening. At the five Horst gave him a hip, spinning him around so completely that the guy actually toppled over.

Touchdown Lincoln!

Ninety-six yards in three plays.

Lincoln was less than two minutes from victory.

Kenstowicz boomed the kickoff down into the right corner. The Lakes returner muffed it, picked it up, took a step, and that's when Angel and about four other guys hit him. Somehow he held on to the football, but Lakes was backed up on their own ten-yard line with a little over a minute and one time-out.

The Lakes fans rose to their feet, screaming "Go Lancers!" so loud that the words rocked back and forth inside the T-Dome. Lincoln went into a prevent defense, and Lakes moved the ball upfield. Only they moved too slowly. They had no gamebreakers, and with every five- or eight-yard gain, twenty to thirty seconds ticked off the clock. Lakes was at their own forty-five, out of time-outs, with nine seconds left. Their quarterback didn't have the arm strength to heave a Hail Mary pass anywhere near the end zone, so they tried the hook-and-ladder play. For a second, it looked as if it might work, but only for a second. When the Lakes receiver was forced out of bounds shy of the thirty, the scoreboard clock read 00:00.

Lincoln was headed to the state championship game.

10

THE LAKES FANS FILED OUT QUICKLY, but like every other Lincoln fan, I stayed in my seat as the team milled around in front of the stands, the band playing and the cheerleaders leading yells and doing flips. Finally McNulty herded the team off the field, which was the signal for everyone else to leave.

As I made my way out of the arena, Lincoln kids started screaming, wild, loud rock-concert screams of pure joy that echoed in the stairwells. It was mainly guys who were screaming, but the electricity was everywhere. Parents and kids, A-students and near dropouts, rich and poor— you could feel the adrenaline rush. Out in the parking lot, car horns blared.

Instead of leaving the Tacoma Dome, I headed over to Gate G-1, the gate where the players exited. Now that the game was over, the fever had left me. And my mind switched right back on. Was Kimi right? Had we missed something?

G-1 opened up to a brightly lit runway with high concrete walls on both sides that funneled players and coaches to the parking lot. I waited at the end of the runway, hoping to see Angel. Players trickled out in groups of three or four, some laughing, most quiet. I saw Horst and Westwood, Price and Blake Stein. Then the door stayed closed for three or four minutes. The temperature was dropping fast; the forecast had been for snow or freezing rain—unusual for Seattle in November. I was about to return to my car when the door opened a final time and Angel and Coach McNulty emerged. They walked about ten feet and stopped and faced each other. They spoke quietly, both of them so intent that neither saw me, although I couldn't have been more than fifty feet away. For a moment I thought of confronting them, right then and there, but instead I slipped back into the darkness of the parking lot. The championship game was a week away; I had time.

I returned to my car, quickly made my way out of the nearly empty lot, and was soon back onto I-5 driving to Seattle. I turned on the CD player, but it was all noise. After a few miles, I flicked it off and listened to the silence.

After forty minutes, I reached Seattle. From the freeway I had another fifteen minutes of driving before I was upstairs in my room. I flicked the TV on and then clicked from stupid station to stupid station. I was watching golf when my cell rang.

"Did McNulty call?" It was Kimi.

"No, but he will."

"You'll tell me when he does, won't you? You won't do anything without me?"

"We're partners," I said.

"I know. I'm just nervous."

"So am I."

There was a long pause. "I hope you won't be mad that I'm telling you this," she finally said, "but when Rachel saw you today, she said she wasn't sure it was you. She said you didn't look overweight at all."

Can you be proud and ashamed at the same time? Because that's how I felt.

"Mitch, are you still there?"

"Yeah, I'm here." I paused. "I'm really tired, Kimi. I think I'm going to call it a night."

THE FORECAST WAS ON TARGET. When I woke up at six on Sunday morning, two inches of pure white snow covered streets and rooftops, lawns and sidewalks. I drove slowly down empty streets to the Ballard Locks and took my normal run, veering off at Elmore so I could see Angel's house. The snow made everything eerily quiet.

Angel's place looked more like a fortress than ever, and it wasn't just because of the iron bars over every window. From under the eaves, spotlights, ineffective in the morning light, shone pointlessly in every direction. I could feel a security system, imagine motion detectors, multiple dead bolts on the front and back doors.

As I ran back to the Locks, I searched for some missing

piece of the puzzle. Back in August, Horst had told me he wasn't afraid of anything. Would Angel say that? I didn't think so. But what was he afraid of? When I reached the bridge, I peered into the ravine. The heron's nests stood out, snow-covered, in the bare trees.

Back at the car, I checked my cell phone: one new voice message. I hit the button, waited for the robot voice to finish, and then heard McNulty's voice. "Call me."

I took a deep breath before hitting redial. McNulty picked up on the first ring. "We have to talk. Face-to-face."

"Okay. How about Peet's?"

"No, not Peet's. Hattie's Hat at ten. See you there."

Before my grandfather died, he'd take me to Hattie's Hat for a hamburger when he visited. He liked it because they served the same food, cooked the same way, every time. Bacon and eggs, hash browns, white toast, and coffee from a percolator. "The menu hasn't changed in one hundred years," he used to say. Probably some of the waitresses have been there one hundred years, too. McNulty wanted to meet on his ground.

I called Kimi. "Can you pick me up?" she asked.

The hours crawled that morning, but finally it was time. Kimi was standing in front of her house, picking at her nails. It can be tough finding parking near Hattie's Hat, but a pickup truck was pulling out of a spot as I turned the corner onto Ballard Avenue.

There's been no smoking allowed in restaurants in Seattle for at least ten years, but so much smoke had oozed into the walls of Hattie's Hat in its first ninety years that the place still reeked of Marlboros. I looked around and spotted McNulty sipping coffee in a booth in the back. Angel wasn't with him.

Kimi and I walked over and slid in across the table from him. A gray-haired waitress with her hair in a bun came by. "Coffee?"

I nodded and she poured me a cup.

"What kind of tea do you have?" Kimi asked.

"Regular tea, sweetie," she said.

"Okay, I'll take that."

"Anything to eat?"

I looked to Kimi, and she gave her head a slight shake. "Maybe later," I said.

After the waitress had hurried off to get Kimi's tea, I put on my best reporter's face and faced McNulty. "Before we start, I want it understood that everything is on the record."

He screwed up his face. "What?"

"On the record. Whatever you say I can use in a story."

McNulty shook his head. "Oh, kid, you are so lost."

"You can insult me all you want," I said, trying to talk myself into a confidence I didn't feel. "It doesn't matter. I've got Angel's history from the *Philadelphia Inquirer.* He played four years at Aramingo High. And he was a quarterback, just like we said the first day when you pretended you didn't know him. But you knew all about his past because you had pulled his records. You knew he wasn't eligible, but you played him anyway because you want to win so badly you're willing to cheat. Those are the facts, and after the *Seattle Times* prints my article, Lincoln will forfeit every game, the title game will be canceled, and you'll lose your job."

I don't know what I expected. That his face would turn red, that he'd start spluttering, denying everything, or maybe that he'd reach across the table and grab me by the throat and start choking me. Instead, he slumped back in his chair, a look of disgust on his face. "That's what you think this is about? Me using Angel to cheat my way to a state title?"

I nodded. "That's exactly what I think this is about."

"And this person you talked to at Aramingo High. Did you tell him that Angel was going to school here?"

"Yes. Why shouldn't I?"

He shook his head. "You have no idea what you've done."

"Explain it to me," I said, coolly.

"First, tell me this. Who was this person at Aramingo? A teacher or a student?"

"A student."

"What was his name?"

Kimi nudged me, and I knew why. McNulty was taking control of the interview. "Look, Mr. McNulty," I said, putting strength into my voice. "His name doesn't matter. If I've missed something, tell me. If not, I'm going to take my story and Kimi's pictures to the *Times*."

He laughed mockingly. "If you missed something? You missed everything."

"You said that before, but you still haven't told me what it is I missed. If you've got some new facts, I'm listening. Otherwise . . ." I opened my hands, palms to the ceiling.

He reached into his back pocket and took out his wallet. From it, he pulled a newspaper clipping. He carefully unfolded the clipping and then slid it between Kimi and me. "Read this," he said.

It was an old op-ed article from the *Philadelphia Inquirer* detailing all the school-age kids who'd been killed during the school year. There'd been twenty-three total. Most were homicides that happened in neighborhoods or in homes. Guns, drugs, gangs.

When I finished reading the article, I looked to Kimi. She nodded that she'd finished it too, so I slid it back to McNulty. "Okay, Philadelphia has some terrible neighborhoods, worse than anything around here. I don't blame Angel for leaving. But just because Philadelphia has problems doesn't make him eligible to play here."

McNulty turned the paper around and slid it back to me. "Read these two paragraphs again," he said. "From here to the end."

I shrugged and then reread the paragraphs.

There were at least two dozen witnesses on Aramingo Avenue when ten-year-old Thomas Childress was shot during a battle between two gangs. One of the witnesses actually braved gunfire to pick young Thomas up from the street and carry him to the sidewalk, but Thomas died before medics reached him. After the shootout, none of the witnesses would speak to police investigators, because—well, we all know why. These thugs carry guns, and it's bad for your health to snitch on them.

But the wall of silence in the terrorized neighborhood has crumbled. The same young man who picked up the bleeding boy from the street has now picked the boy's killers from a lineup. Because of his courage Assistant Attorney General Lynne Fox will be able to prosecute the case. "To come

forward, to step up and speak up—it's the moral thing to do, the right thing to do," Ms. Fox told assembled media. "Now we have someone who has had the courage to do it. I wish I had a dozen willing witnesses in a dozen other cases, but at least I have one, and one's a start."

I slid the paper back to him. "All right, I read it twice. I still don't get it."

"Who do you think picked the boy up from the street? Who do you think testified against the killers in court?"

I could feel beads of sweat on my forehead, but I forced myself to smile. "Come on. You're not trying to tell me it was Angel Marichal, are you? You think I'm going to believe that?"

McNulty kept staring at me, and my head started spinning so fast, I grabbed hold of the tabletop to keep from falling to the floor.

12

OUR WAITRESS RETURNED. "Your tea, sweetie," she said, placing a stainless steel pitcher of boiling water, a mug, and a Lipton tea bag in front of Kimi.

"Thank you," Kimi said, without looking up.

The waitress looked at me. "More coffee?"

I nodded and she refilled my cup and then McNulty's.

Once the waitress had moved to another table, Kimi tapped the article with her finger. "If the person in this story is Angel, how did he end up in Seattle?" She was trying to sound professional, but her voice quavered.

McNulty leaned forward, so close that I could feel his anger. "The person you saw with him the first day of practice—that's a cousin. When the trial ended, Angel moved in with him to get out of harm's way in Philly. Angel needs two more credits to get a diploma. When he graduates, there's a college that'll give him a football scholarship. I'm not telling you which college, so don't ask, but it's a safe place, a place where guys from Philly would never think to look.

"Once Angel enrolled at Lincoln, his football coach from Aramingo High called me. He said reclaiming that stolen season would mean everything to Angel, and he asked me if I could somehow get Angel onto my team. I checked with the Washington State Athletic Association—I'm not a cheater and I never was, in spite of the rumors—and they gave me the go-ahead. I've kept Angel below the radar to be on the safe side. But because of you two, those gang guys back in Philadelphia now know he goes to Lincoln High, and when you get your precious article published, everybody in the country will know."

"That's not fair," Kimi said. "We didn't know any of this. Besides, we haven't published anything."

"Not yet you haven't," McNulty said, looking right at me. "But you can still go to Chet the Jet. It's not the story you thought you had, but it's still one helluva story. You'll make quite a splash, and that's what this is all about, right?"

He was right. It was a great story, and there was nothing to stop us from publishing it. I could rework what I'd written and the *Times* would jump at it: *Hero Makes Most of Second Chance.*

I looked to Kimi. How much did making a name for herself matter to her? Our eyes met, and she gave her head a small shake. I turned back to McNulty. "We won't go to Chet the Jet, or to anyone. Not unless Angel says we can."

"That'll never happen," McNulty said.

"Then we'll never publish," I said.

McNulty's eyes shifted to Kimi.

"I won't tell anyone," she said.

He smoothed his napkin with his fingertips. "Now I need to ask you a couple of things. Things that matter for Angel's immediate safety."

"Go ahead," I said.

"The guy in Philadelphia—his name?"

"He wouldn't tell me."

"He knows Angel goes to Lincoln, but what else does he know?"

"Nothing."

"You didn't give him Angel's home address? Angel's cousin told me you've been around his place."

"He wanted Angel's address, but I didn't give it to him."

"You're sure? Because if you did, tell me so I can get Angel out of there."

"I'm positive."

"All right, last thing. This guy—how did he sound to you? Gut feeling."

My heart drummed in my chest. "Dangerous."

McNulty's jaw tightened. He took out his wallet and dropped a five-dollar bill and two ones onto the table. "This is on me," he said, and then he left.

Kimi finished her tea, and I finished my coffee. The waitress picked up our cups along with McNulty's money. "You can keep the change," I said.

"Thanks, honey."

After we trudged back to the car through the snow, I drove Kimi home. The sidewalks and lawns were white, but the heat from the car engines had turned the streets into gray slush. When I pulled up in front of Kimi's house, she stepped out of the car. Instead of closing the door and going inside, she leaned back toward me. "Gang guys don't forget, Mitch. They're all about payback. They'll kill him if they get a chance."

"Kimi, Philadelphia is three thousand miles away. They don't know where Angel lives. It's not like they have an American Express credit card and they're going to use it to fly out here, rent a hotel room, rent a car, and then drive around looking for him."

She stood holding the door for a long time. "We missed something before," she finally said. "What if we're missing something again?"

PART FIVE

I

I **DIDN'T WANT TO GO HOME,** so I drove down to the Ballard Locks and walked out to the fish ladder. The salmon runs had ended, so the underground viewing room was deserted. I sat on one of the benches staring at the green, lifeless water.

My mind circled back to the article McNulty had shown me. I'd read the words and I'd understood what had happened, but only in my brain. Now, as I sat shivering in the cold, the words turned into images. And as the images grew stronger, I started to feel what had happened.

I could picture little kids walking to school, dragging their backpacks along the sidewalk, talking to friends. And then, in the street, two cars coming at each other from opposite directions. Both cars slow as they see each other. The closer they get, the slower they go, until they stop, side by side. The drivers roll down their windows. They talk a little, and then the talk turns to shouting and

233

swearing. The little kids look over, scared but interested. That's when a hand holding a gun comes out of the window. *Tat! Tat! Tat! Tat!* And now more guns, more *Tat! Tat! Tat! Tat!* The little kids start screaming, start hiding behind cars. But one, Thomas Childress, is crossing the street when the guns start firing. He tries to run for cover, but a bullet strikes him and he goes down.

That's when Angel runs out, bullets still flying, screaming, "Stop! Stop! Stop!" And the gang guys speed away, tires screeching, heading in opposite directions. Angel carries Thomas to the sidewalk. He lays him down and presses his hand against Thomas's skull to stop the flow of blood. He's waiting to hear the siren of an ambulance. Somebody must have called. Why is it taking so long? But it's no good—there's no stopping the blood. Angel feels the life go out of Thomas.

Everybody in the neighborhood knows the cars, knows who was in the cars. They want to get the thugs off the streets, but they're afraid. The police come around: "I didn't see . . . I wasn't there . . . I can't be sure."

Only Angel stands up. He points out the killers from a lineup and he points them out again in the courtroom. "It was him and him and him and him."

"We're gonna get you," one of the gang guys shouts as they take him, shackled and wearing an orange jumpsuit, off to prison. "You can't hide from us. You're gonna die. You're gonna die."

I stared at the water for a long time, thinking how close I'd come to giving Angel away. Finally the cold was too much. I wanted to go home, lie down on my bed, pull the covers over my head, and sleep—but there was something I had to do first.

Angel.

Face-to-face, I had to see him.

I returned to the car and drove through the slushy streets to his house. I parked and looked up the walkway to the front windows. The blinds were drawn, but as I watched, a finger separated them.

I got out, walked to the front door, pulled the screen door open, and knocked. The door opened immediately; Angel was on the other side, his cousin two steps behind him.

"I'm Mitch True."

"I know who you are," Angel answered.

"And I know who you are . . . now. I know what you did in Philadelphia. I didn't before. Before today, I thought—" I stopped. What did it matter what I thought?

"Why are you here?"

I took a breath. "I guess to say that I'm sorry." I stopped, but he just stared, his face blank. I felt desperate. "And to let you know that if there's anything I can do, I'll do it. Just tell me and I swear to God, I'll do it."

"You know what you can do?" he said, his voice expressionless. "You can leave me alone."

The door closed in my face.

I returned to the car and sat, my hands on the steering wheel. What had I expected? Did I think he was going to tell me it wasn't my fault, and then toss a football around with me? I started the car and drove away.

I'd gone about three blocks when my cell phone rang. I looked at the screen: Chet the Jet. I let it go to voice mail. When I got home, I did what I'd wanted to do earlier. I went upstairs, closed the door, turned off the light, and slept.

2

WHEN I AWOKE, I wondered if I'd slept through the night. I used my cell phone to check the time: 2:30 p.m. I sat up, but still nothing seemed right. Had I really met with McNulty, with Angel? So much had happened.

My cell phone chirped at me. I hit a button and the screen lit up. *Four Missed Calls.* Two were from area code 215—Philadelphia. I wasn't calling that guy back.

The other two were from Chet the Jet. I didn't want to talk to him, but I knew he'd just keep calling. I hit *Call back,* and he answered on the first ring.

"What's going on, Mitch?" he said, his voice edgy.

"What do you mean?"

"I mean I got a call from a guy asking for Bob Bernstein, the reporter who covers the Lincoln Mustangs. You have any idea who Bob Bernstein might be?"

"No," I said, fighting to keep my voice level.

"No? That's interesting. Because right after he asked about Bernstein, he asked about Angel Marichal, which made me think that Bob Bernstein just might be Mitch True."

"Did you tell him that?" I asked, fighting down the panic.

"I told him nothing, which is when he started threatening me, saying I had to tell him where Angel lives or else. He did not sound like a nice person. So I'm asking you again, Mitch Bernstein: What's going on?"

"Nothing's going on."

He laughed, an angry laugh. "I was at the Lakes game; I saw Marichal play. For the first time all year I saw him. I spent this morning watching tapes of Lincoln's games. What you wrote about him—it was on the money. The stat sheets Coach Morris has been sending me are garbage.

Now, Morris wouldn't feed me lies unless McNulty told him to, and McNulty wouldn't do that unless he had a reason. Do you know what the reason is?"

"No."

"No idea?"

"I don't know anything."

"I've been a reporter for thirty years. I can tell when someone is lying, and you're lying. So let me lay out the situation for you. You work for the *Seattle Times*. Something doesn't smell right about Angel Marichal. I don't know what's causing the stench, and maybe you don't know everything, but you've got ideas. You tell me what you know, I'll take it from there, and if it comes to something, we'll share a byline."

"I don't know anything," I repeated.

"That's it? Final answer?"

"That's it."

His voice went ice cold. "Wrong answer. Unless you call me back with a better one, you're finished with the *Times*. No basketball stories, no baseball stories. The summer internship you were hoping for? Gone. And don't even think about asking for a letter of recommendation for whatever fancy-ass college you want to go to. Goodbye."

3

THE AFTERNOON CRAWLED INTO EVENING. I wished my parents were home so that I could hear them moving around downstairs, but I knew they'd stay late at their office. Snow always messed up deliveries.

Around six I went down to the kitchen, flipped through the newspaper, and half watched the Sunday night football game for an hour. Then I microwaved a frozen pasta dinner, ate it in front of the TV, returned to my room, propped up some pillows on the bed, and sat there, my legs stretched out in front of me.

My parents came in around nine. I went downstairs and heard all about a delivery truck that had slid into a ditch in Shoreline. As I listened, I thought of my dad saying I could talk to him at any time. I wanted to talk to him now, but I couldn't think of a place to begin. By nine thirty I was back in my room looking out the window. Snow was falling, and the forecast was for snow all night. There'd be no school Monday.

I fell asleep quickly. I had about a million dreams that night, but I remember only one: I was back at the Tacoma Dome. The title game had ended; the parking lot was emptying out. I was waiting by the players' gate for Angel, just as I'd waited after the semifinals. I had a notebook with a long list of questions for him, but as I looked at the questions, the words somehow morphed into a foreign language that looked like Russian.

The players' door opened and guys started spilling out, walking down the long, brightly lit chute to the parking lot. I knew I should ask somebody something, but I couldn't think what.

I was about to leave when the door opened a final time and Angel stepped out, alone. He started toward me, down that walkway. *What do I want to ask him?* And then, like a miracle, the questions in my notebook morphed back into English. At that exact moment a car pulled up at the end of the long chute. The car had a Washington license plate—I remember that detail as clearly as everything that followed. The window came down. A hand holding a gun appeared. *Tat! Tat! Tat! Tat!* Then the car was speeding off toward Interstate 5; Angel was down on the ground just like Thomas Childress had been, his blood staining the concrete, and I was sitting up in my bed sweating from every pore of my body.

I'd never get back to sleep, so even though it was a little before six a.m., I put on about four layers of clothes and headed out into the frozen morning, making the first footsteps in the white snow as I walked up to Sunset Hill

Park. I stared out over Puget Sound until the first rays of the sun lit up the peaks of the Olympic Mountains. There was something more than terror in that dream, some detail that gnawed at me. What was it?

Frustrated, I grabbed hold of the chain-link fence and gave it a shake. Snow cascaded from the little wires where it had settled. Then, out of nowhere, I knew. The Washington license plates. In my dream those plates had been as vivid as the gunshots. But knowing *what* detail mattered only increased my frustration. Why did it matter? I had no answer.

I turned and headed for home. I'd gone about one hundred yards when I stopped in my tracks. My phone call to Aramingo High . . . what had the guy said to me? *"We've got some homeboys out there who are going to pay him a visit."*

Homeboys in Seattle.

The Washington license plates in my dream.

Nobody had to fly in from Philadelphia. The Aramingo guys were connected to a Seattle gang; it was Seattle guys who'd be coming after Angel.

I hurried home, frustrated that the snow slowed me. By the time I was back in the house, it was nearly eight. I didn't know whether Kimi would be up, but I called anyway. She answered right away. "You're going to have to make it quick."

"Okay, I'll be as quick as I can. Remember what you said about missing something?"

Then I described my dream and repeated the words the Philly guy had said to me over the phone. The phone stayed quiet. I waited. "Kimi?"

"I remember the walkway by G-1," she said. "I remember thinking that it was perfect for photographers because it was bright and there was no place to hide. If gang guys figure out Angel's playing in the Tacoma Dome on Saturday night, they can get him. There's a big sign that says PLAYERS ONLY. They'd have to be blind to miss it. Going in or coming out—they can get him."

"So what do we do?"

"Call McNulty. Tell him what you told me. Tell him Angel can't play."

"All right, I will. And then I'll call you right back."

"That won't work, Mitch. I'm going out for breakfast with my father and my aunt; they're in the car waiting for me right now. Besides, I think we should talk." There was a pause. "Okay, I've got it. I'm meeting Rachel at the library at ten thirty to study for a chemistry test. See if you can get one of those study rooms. I'll meet you there at ten."

4

AFTER I HUNG UP, I took a shower and ate a cup of yogurt, mainly to let some time pass. I figured Coach McNulty was keeping late hours preparing a game plan. I didn't want to be the one to wake him. At nine, I called. The phone rang four times before he answered.

"What do you want, Mitch?" His voice sounded annoyed.

"There's something I didn't tell you at Hattie's Hat, something important."

"So tell me."

"The Philadelphia guy. He's got connections in Seattle. That time I talked to him, he said . . ." I raced through my explanation, knowing that I was talking too fast, but unable to slow myself. When I finished, I expected McNulty to ask me questions, but he didn't say a word. "This matters, doesn't it?" I said. "A connection with Seattle gangs makes everything more dangerous, right?"

"I don't see how," McNulty said. "You didn't give Angel's address to anybody, right?"

"I didn't. I know I didn't."

"Then nothing has changed. Angel's not coming back to Lincoln and there's no way they'll find his house."

"But there's something else," I said quickly, "something that goes with it."

"I'm listening."

For the second time, I described how easy it would be for some gang guy to drive a car to the end of the walkway at the Tacoma Dome, stick a gun out the window and fire, and then lose himself on the freeway.

"Mitch, there's not a chance in the world anybody is going to try anything at the game. Police and security guys will be all around the Tacoma Dome. They'd never get away with it. I'm not yanking Angel off the field because of some vague feeling that—"

"It's more than a vague feeling," I said.

"No, it isn't. You've got no names, no car license number, no reason to think anything is going to happen." He stopped, and when he spoke again his voice was controlled. "Listen to me. You feel guilty about Philadelphia. Okay, I understand. You want to do something to make up for it. I understand that, too. But this is your last phone call to me. Everything is under control, so stop playing Sherlock Holmes."

The phone went dead.

I bundled up and headed to the library. I thought it would be empty, but the snowfall had driven the homeless guys inside, and young mothers had brought their little kids, too. Lynn Miller is the librarian there, and she knows me. I asked her if there were any study rooms available.

"Technically no," she said, "but the woman who signed up for Room C isn't here. The snow might keep her at home. I'll let you use it, but if she does show up, you'll have to leave."

I took Room C and texted Kimi where I was. Five minutes later she was sitting across a study table from me. She took her gloves off and blew into her hands to warm them. "What did McNulty say?"

"That there will be police and security guys all around."

"So he's going to let him play?"

I nodded.

"But that's crazy."

"Maybe," I said. "But maybe not."

"What's that supposed to mean?"

"McNulty thinks I'm making stuff up because I feel guilty about blowing Angel's cover."

"And you buy that?"

"I'm not sure. I don't have anything concrete. No names or description of a suspicious car. It's all based on a dream."

Kimi put her hands flat on the table. "I'm going to talk to my father, tell him everything. He'll know what we should do."

My eyes widened. Her father? The funny little Asian man with his garden hoe and his rows of perfect petunias. What would he know about gangs?

"Why are you looking at me like that?" she said.

I chose my words carefully. "Kimi, your dad is a bright man, but this takes street smarts, not book smarts."

"You don't know anything about my father."

"I know he's not in a gang."

"How do you think we got to America?" she asked, her mouth set.

"You told me Microsoft hired him."

"Microsoft brought us here from Seoul, yes. But I was born in North Korea."

It was my turn to be surprised. "How did you get out? I didn't think anybody ever got out of North Korea."

"You want to know? Okay, I'll tell you."

It happened when she was five. Her family lived way north in some city with a strange name I can't remember. They just took off one day: her father, her mother, her aunt, and Kimi. She described long train rides, long walks under cover of darkness, lots of hiding during the day. And then, just before they were to cross into South Korea, they were caught.

"We were in a warehouse by a river," she told me. "I was

lying down behind sacks of rice. A soldier came in, his flashlight playing over the burlap sacks. The light fell on my mother, and he shot her. Not a word of warning. He just shot her. My dad jumped out and hit him. The soldier fell, and my dad hit him over and over. I still remember the sound. Finally the hitting stopped; the soldier was still. My father motioned, and we followed him out of the warehouse. It was twilight, nearly dark. He led us across a field to a riverbank. He pointed to the other side and we stepped into the river. It was shallow, but moving very fast. Halfway across, the current caught me and I lost my balance. I thought I was going to drown, but my father grabbed me. After what seemed like forever, we were on the other side, safe. My aunt, my father, and me—but not my mother."

When she finished, I just sat, looking at the table. What could I say? Seconds ticked away. "I'm sorry," I said at last. I waited. "You're right, Kimi. Talk to your father."

She nodded toward the small window. "Rachel's here."

I stood and headed toward the door.

"Let's meet in the commons before school tomorrow," she said.

"There won't be school, not with all this snow," I said.

"I heard a forecast. It's supposed to get twenty degrees warmer and rain all night. There'll be school."

5

THE RAIN BEGAN AROUND EIGHT and kept on falling all Monday night. By Tuesday morning every trace of snow was gone. I arrived at Lincoln High half an hour early. The cheer squad must have worked through the snow day decorating the school. Posters were taped on doors and along hallways. Black and red streamers hung from the ceilings of every hallway and all through the commons. Banners reading GO LINCOLN! fluttered from classroom windows.

When I pushed open the door into the commons, I spotted Kimi sitting at a back table, her face tired, her hair pulled back into a haphazard ponytail. "What did your father say?" I asked once I took a chair across from her.

"He says we should think the way gangs think."

"What does that mean?"

She leaned toward me. "What do these guys know about Angel?"

I thought for a moment. "They know that he goes to Lincoln and that he's on the football team."

"That's not much, which is why they won't wait until the night of the championship game to make their first move. My dad is sure they'll come to Lincoln High looking for him."

"But they won't find him. McNulty's keeping Angel away from school and out of practices. So there's no problem."

"Don't you see, Mitch? They won't find Angel, but we could find them. If we figure out who's after Angel, we could pass a license plate number to the police. If we had something solid, the police would pay attention."

"There are hundreds of cars here every day. How will we spot them?"

"Those guys up at the Moonlite Mini-Mart found us, and it didn't take them long. We didn't fit in. So we look for gang guys hanging around Lincoln, guys who don't fit in. We can take turns. I'll cut first, third, and fifth periods. You can cut second, fourth, and sixth. We can walk around, or hang out across the street from school, or sit at a window table at Zestos." She paused. "Look, I know it's a long shot, but I can't stand doing nothing. And if we don't see any strange cars, we'll feel better, won't we?"

"Okay, we'll do it. Only I'll take first period. You've got a test coming up in chemistry."

6

WHEN THE FIRST BELL SOUNDED, I walked out of the school and across the street. It felt strange to be outside during class hours. Groups of kids milled about, smoking and talking, but I avoided eye contact. My plan was to walk the perimeter of the school a few times, go to Zestos for coffee, and then walk the perimeter a couple more times, my eyes taking in everything, though what I wanted to see was nothing.

I'd crossed the street and started toward the athletic fields when a voice called out to me. "You cutting class, Mitchie?" It was purple-haired Laurie Walloch. She was sitting, cigarette in hand, on a four-foot retaining wall in front of a condo development on which all work had stopped.

I smiled. "Actually, yeah, I am."

She blew out a long stream of blue smoke. "I never thought a good boy like you would cut class. You want one?" Laurie held out her package of cigarettes.

"No, but thanks."

I started off, and then I realized that Laurie spent more time outside the school than in it. If there was a strange car cruising the area, she'd spot it way before I would. I turned back. "I'm not really cutting."

Laurie smiled. "It's okay, Mitch. I won't tell your mom."

"No, really. I'm actually looking for some gang guys who might be cruising the school. Maybe you could help."

"What kind of car?" she asked.

"That's it. I don't know."

"What's this about?" Laurie said, interested in something for once.

"It's for a story. I'm on the school newspaper."

"That's cool, Mitch. Kind of a mystery. I'll keep my eyes open."

"Thanks," I said, and then another thought came. "You don't spend all day outside, do you? You go to some classes, right?"

"Mornings I hang out here. If I get real cold, I go there." She nodded toward the half-built condos. "Most days I eat lunch in the commons, and in the afternoons I take pottery and then Navigation 101 with Ms. Laird. But don't worry—if these guys come around, I'll spot them."

I left Laurie and walked around the school, feeling awkward and out of place. After I finished my circuit, I spent forty minutes at Zestos sipping a cup of coffee and listening to fifties music played way too loud through speakers way too old to handle the volume. Before the hour ended, I checked back with Laurie. "Nothing," she said.

I returned to the school. As I was heading in, Kimi was coming out. "You won't have to cut any morning classes," I said, pulling her to the side and explaining about Laurie.

"Do you think she'll pay attention? She sounds spacy."

"She'll pay attention. And she won't stick out like you and I would. If somebody is hunting for Angel, and they see you or me on the sidewalk, watching, they'll notice us. Laurie belongs out there."

I couldn't pay attention in my morning classes. I felt lightheaded, as if I hadn't eaten in a week. I wondered if Kimi was able to focus any better. At lunchtime I met up with her in the hall, and we went together to check with Laurie.

As soon as Laurie saw us, she came off her perch by the condo, flicked a cigarette to the ground, and grinned. "I think I saw your guys," she said, her voice excited. "Between second and third period, and then again between third and fourth. A black Honda Civic hatchback with tinted windows. They might have been here last week, too. They cruised really slow, but the weird thing is that they had no music going, and it's the kind of car with the kind of guys that you'd expect to really rock. They were checking out everybody who came out of the building. Once the passing period ended and kids headed back into the school, they were out of here. There!" she said, pointing. "There they are now."

My knees felt as if they were made out of Jell-O, but somehow I managed to turn and watch a Civic creep slowly past the Lincoln High parking lot. The windows facing the parking lot were down an inch or two; the other two windows—the windows facing us—were tightly shut.

Once the Civic passed the parking lot, it sped up, raced around the block, and then made another silent pass, again slowly inching its way. I couldn't see the guys inside, but I could feel their eyes scanning the groups of kids, searching. I looked to Kimi; her face was pale.

On the second pass, just before the car sped off, I remembered the license number. I looked, preparing to commit the numbers and letters to memory, but instead of real plates the Civic had a temporary license taped to the back window. Worse, the tape had come loose, and the temporary license had half slipped. All I could see were the letters *RZ*. Maybe the third letter was *T*, but it might have been *F* or even *B*. I couldn't read any of the numbers. And then the car sped up again, down the block and away.

"Those are your guys, right?" Laurie said, smiling.

"You've never seen that car before?" Kimi asked.

Laurie looked her over. "You're Kimi something, right?"

"Kimi Yon."

Laurie grinned at her. "You got a thing for Mitch, Kimi?" She turned to me. "Mitch, you got a girl? You lost weight, didn't you?"

"We work together on stories for the newspaper. She's the photographer and I'm the writer."

"Have you seen that car before?" Kimi asked again.

"I told you—not before last week," Laurie answered. Then she paused. "What's this really about, anyway? Both of you look kind of sick."

Kimi and I returned to the school. We had a few minutes before fifth period began, so we ducked into the newspaper office. Kimi plunked herself down on the old sofa; I sat in the oversize chair. "Did you notice the license plate?" I asked.

"I saw it," she said, her eyes on the carpet. "Or maybe I should say I didn't see it."

"Do you think it was that way on purpose?"

"I don't know. Maybe."

That night my parents worked late again. I microwaved a frozen chicken dinner and ate alone. Later, as I was heading upstairs, the phone rang. I went into my dad's small office to answer. "Is this the True residence?" a male voice asked. He sounded like one of my parents' delivery drivers calling to say he was quitting.

"Yeah, this is the True residence, but my parents aren't home. Can I take a message?"

"Are you Mitch True?"

"Yeah, I'm Mitch. Is there a message?"

Instead of answering, whoever it was cut the connection.

Immediately I hit *Call back* to retrieve the number. What I didn't want to see was a Philadelphia area code. What I saw were the words *Private Party,* and that was no better.

How could they have traced me? It wasn't possible. And then I saw the answer right in front of me. My dad's fax machine. I'd used it to send the photo of Angel to that guy in Philadelphia, and he'd used a reverse dictionary to find me. If he could get my home phone number, he could get my address.

My mom and dad came home about an hour later. I went down and talked with them a little. Before I returned to my room, I double-checked the dead bolt on both the front and back doors.

7

BEFORE SCHOOL ON WEDNESDAY, I found Laurie Walloch in her normal spot. She was sharing a smoke with her friend Lynn. "You going to be out here this morning?" I asked.

"Yeah, sure. Where else?" Laurie answered.

I gave her my cell number. "If the Civic shows up, text me. Okay?"

"Okay," Laurie said, "but only because you've always been nice to me. I'm not liking the feel of this."

All morning I waited for my cell phone to vibrate, but it never did. I kept thinking about how stupid I'd been to tell the Juan Doe guy that Angel went to Lincoln High. If I'd kept my mouth shut, he'd have had no chance of tracking Angel down—and no reason to track me down, either. At lunch I checked with Laurie and Lynn. "No Honda Civic," Laurie said, blowing on the ash of her cigarette. "Just a normal day."

Laurie and Lynn went into Lincoln for their afternoon classes, so I cut fifth period and stayed outside. No black Civic hatchback. Kimi cut sixth while I went to class. No black Civic hatchback.

Thursday played out the same: no Civic in the morning, no Civic in the afternoon. I told myself not to worry. The guys in the Civic weren't after Angel. They had no ties with Philadelphia. They were just cruising Lincoln, probably hoping to pick up girls. Everything was going to be all right.

Friday morning I sleepwalked through my first three

periods. Fourth period was canceled for a pep rally before lunch. The local TV stations had crews out, and enough students showed up to fill the gym. Down on the basketball court McNulty had his players sitting on gray folding chairs under the north basket. I scanned the faces twice, afraid that I'd see Angel, but he wasn't there. I breathed a sigh of relief. Kimi was on the gym floor, too, taking photos for the *Lincoln Light*.

The assembly opened with the school president reciting the Pledge of Allegiance while all the kids in the bleachers talked. Then the lights went off, and the librarian showed a ten-minute highlight film some parent—probably Horst's mother—had put together. Next the cheer team came out and did flips while the band played Lincoln's fight song. After that, the vice principal, Bertha Brown, took the podium. "Other Lincoln High clubs and programs have also done well this fall, and we need to honor them. The chess club placed—"

That's when my cell phone vibrated. I pulled it out and flipped it open. I'd gotten a two-word text from Laurie Walloch: BLACK CIVIC.

For a moment I sat paralyzed. But then I searched the gym floor for Kimi. She was crouched, her back to me, taking pictures of the chess players as they received medals. I looked to the stage area and saw at least twenty more kids waiting to get some plaque or ribbon. She wouldn't look back toward me for five or ten minutes, at least. I couldn't wait.

I worked my way out of the bleachers and exited the gym through a side door. A minute later I was across the street. As soon as I caught Laurie Walloch's eye, she looked east, toward the baseball field. I followed her gaze and saw the Civic, gliding slowly down the street.

I needed the license number. With it, I could go to McNulty. If he didn't do anything, I could go to the police myself. Would the Civic make another circuit of the school, or was this my last chance?

I started running. So long as the car didn't speed up, I could catch it. If I was lucky, the temporary license would be taped to the window like it was supposed to be. One good look was all I needed.

For the first fifty yards, I was gaining ground, but then the Civic accelerated. I left the sidewalk to get clear of kids milling around and ran right down the middle of the street. They were pulling away, but then I caught a break. A pickup truck from an intersecting street cut in front of the Civic, forcing it to slow.

I was gaining on it again. I could see the license was properly taped up in the rear window. That made sense too. If the police couldn't see the license, they'd pull those guys over, and they didn't look as though they'd want to be talking to cops about anything. Adrenaline kicked in, pushing me faster and faster. A few more strides and I'd be close enough.

Right then the Civic swung left and abruptly pulled to a stop, brakes squealing. Both doors opened and two guys jumped out. Dark hair, dark glasses, dark clothes. "You chasing us?" the driver shouted, walking toward me.

I stopped. My heart, already racing, went to fast-forward. I shook my head. "No." I looked behind me. The school parking lot was filled with kids, but it was a foot-ball field away. I headed sideways, slipping between two cars and back onto the sidewalk.

One guy was pointing his finger at me. "Come here," the other guy was saying. "We want to talk to you."

I shook my head. "I don't know you," I said, and I turned and started running back toward the parking lot of the school, looking over my shoulder as I ran.

"And you don't want to know us, either," the same guy shouted, taking a couple of steps toward me.

I peeked back over my shoulder every few yards as I ran. They watched me, both of them, until I'd reached the safety of the school parking lot. Then they got back in their car and drove away.

I kept running until I was inside the school. Only then did I stop and catch my breath. I looked up and saw Kimi. Quickly I explained what had happened.

"Why didn't you wait for me?" she said angrily.

"I couldn't, Kimi. There was no time."

"Did you get the license number?"

I shook my head. "They saw me and came after me. There were two of them for sure, and maybe two more in the back. I had to get away fast."

8

After school I did my regular run. I was feeling edgy, and running always shuts down my mind. Only that day it didn't. If I'd just gone a few more steps forward, I'd have seen the license plate. Ten more feet—that was all I'd needed. So what if they'd caught me? They'd have pushed me around a little, maybe even hit me. I'd have come out of it okay, and I'd have had the license number.

That night I ate dinner with my parents and then went to my room. I knew I couldn't study, so I tried to read *Childhood's End,* an old sci-fi book I'd always liked. I'd get

through a couple of pages, but I wouldn't remember anything. Finally, I put the book down.

I thought about calling the police, but what was the
point? Some cop would answer and write stuff down, but
I had no facts. Nothing would come of it. Without McNulty
backing me up, I'd be some crazy kid with a wild imagina-
tion. And there was no point in e-mailing or calling
McNulty again—he'd made that clear.

The cops were out, which left . . . what? How could I stop
a bunch of gangsters? Maybe Kimi's father could face them
down, or Angel, or even Horst. But Mitch True?

My mind went back to the Tacoma Dome and the players' gate. I could see the chute—long and narrow with
high concrete walls on both sides. I knew where the dan-
ger would come from. Angel heading from the stadium
toward the parking lot . . . the black Civic pulling up . . .
the window rolling down, followed by the sounds of gunfire . . . the car speeding off.

My mind stopped right at that phrase.

The car speeding off.

An idea came to me like a bolt of lightning.

I stood up and paced the room, and the idea turned
into a plan. I grabbed the Focus keys from my desk and
hurried downstairs. "Where are you going, Dan?" my mom
asked me as I pulled on my shoes.

"I need to get something at Big Five."

"They close at eight. Why don't you go tomorrow?"

"I'll make it."

It was five to eight when I reached Big 5 Sporting Goods. I pushed the door open and stepped inside.

"Can I help you?" The clerk was just a couple of years older than I was, and I sensed he was afraid I'd hang around past closing time.

"I need a hunting knife," I said, acting as if I'd bought dozens of them. "A good one."

He tilted his head, surprised, but he didn't say anything.

I followed him to the camping section. He stopped, took out some keys, opened a cabinet, reached in, and pulled out a shiny knife with a six-inch blade. "This one is stainless steel, is comfortable in the hand, has excellent safety features, and comes with a nylon belt sheath. It's normally forty dollars, but it's on sale for twenty-five. It's a good all-around knife."

"How about the blade? Is it sharp?"

"It'll cut whatever needs cutting."

I paid, returned to the Focus, and opened the trunk. I lifted up the carpet and put the knife into the black pouch where the jack was kept. Then I closed the trunk and drove home.

9

SATURDAY.

Championship Saturday.

It was all going to end.

Around noon Kimi called. "Can you give me a ride to the game?"

"I thought you were going with Marianne and Rachel."

"I want to get there early to take photos during warm-ups," she said. "Besides, we started this together; we should finish it together."

I picked her up at five thirty. On the drive to Tacoma she asked whether I thought Lincoln would win. Neither of us cared all that much, but it was a way to keep from thinking about the black Civic.

I'd done my research that morning, mainly to make the hours go quicker. Lincoln was playing Ferris High from Spokane. Since Ferris was from eastern Washington, nobody in Seattle knew much about them. I rattled on to Kimi about Ferris's star running back, Micah Pengilly, and how he was headed to Oklahoma, which meant he had to be special. "Adrian Peterson went there," I said, and then realized Kimi had no idea who Adrian Peterson was.

Somewhere past Sea-Tac airport we both fell quiet. I thought she might pull out her iPod; instead she stared out the window. No snow, no rain—just gray and dreary. I paid the parking guy ten dollars and followed the orange cones to the North area and parked in section A, row 8, space 32. There were maybe fifty cars there—parents of players, probably. I looked at my watch—we were ninety minutes early. "I think I'll just walk around for a bit," I said. "You go on in."

"I'm not stupid, Mitch," she said, irritated. "You're looking for the Civic. I'll help."

Neither of us expected to find it, and we didn't. Those guys wouldn't try anything before the game. All the traffic in all the lanes was coming in—they'd be trapped. But after the game, they could go with the flow of traffic, hit the freeway, and be sixty miles away in sixty minutes.

I walked Kimi to the photographers' entrance. "Why don't you watch with me from field level tonight?" she said.

I shook my head. "I wish I could, but I need to be higher up to see the plays and get the numbers right."

She nodded and went inside. Instead of going up to the press entrance on the one hundred level, I headed back to the parking lot.

10

THINK THE WAY GANGS THINK. That's what Kimi's dad had said. I went to the players' gate and looked around. If I were driving the black Civic, where would I park? What would I do?

I scanned the area until I spotted the perfect place: the fence directly across from the players' gate. The Civic could back up against it and wait. From there, the driver could see the players come down the brightly lit chute toward the parking lot without being seen. When he spotted Angel, he could fly down the lane, make a quick right turn, and stop. A passenger in the car could stick a gun out the window, fire, and then the car would be gone, out of the parking lot and onto I-5. Once the Civic reached the freeway, it could head toward Portland or Gig Harbor or Mount Rainier or back to Seattle.

I walked out to the fence. The overhead lighting in the parking lot dwindled to nothing before I reached it. The ground was littered with cups and candy bar wrappers that had blown up against the fence.

I looked back to the players' gate, and I was more certain than ever that this would be where they'd settle. I walked along the fence, kicking glass and garbage out of the way, thinking how stupid I'd been not to bring gloves, and wondering whether, if it finally came to it, I'd have the guts to do what had to be done.

After I'd walked a hundred yards along the fence, I headed back to the T-Dome and found the regular press gate. As I showed the usher my pass, I remembered how awkward I'd felt using it the first time; now it was second nature. I found a seat that was high enough to see everything, but not so high that the players looked like ants.

I looked around me. Cops and security guys were visible throughout the stadium. Coach McNulty had been right. Nobody would be stupid enough to try anything during the game. If an attack came, it would come afterward in the confusion and blackness of the parking lot.

But that was three hours away. I had a football game to cover for the *Lincoln Light,* the most important football game in the history of Lincoln High. Win or lose, students, teachers, and parents would keep the newspaper their whole lives. Over time, my words would become their memories. I opened a new Word document on my laptop, and typed: *Championship Game: Lincoln Mustangs vs. Ferris Saxons.*

II

BEFORE THE TEAMS TOOK THE FIELD, the bands competed. Ferris played a loud, fast "Johnny B. Goode" that Lincoln matched with "Twist and Shout." After that it was "Proud Mary" vs. "Crocodile Rock" and then "Running on Empty" vs. "YMCA." As the songs rolled on, more and more people filed in, and the tension built.

At eight o'clock, the PA announcer introduced the teams. A roar went up for every Lincoln player, but for Horst Diamond the roar was nuclear. Fewer of Ferris's fans had made the long drive from Spokane so they couldn't match Lincoln's volume, but when the name Micah Pengilly was announced, the cheers nearly equaled those for Horst. After the introductions came "The Star-Spangled Banner" followed by the coin toss. Finally, it was game time.

We won the coin toss, which meant we would get the ball first. Forty-four—Angel—trotted onto the field, and as he did I felt my throat tighten. "Let him win," I whispered.

Ferris's kickoff was high and deep. Stein, the return man, muffed it, then picked it up and advanced almost to the thirty before being smacked down. And now it was

Horst running onto the field, and I found myself wanting him to win, too, which is when I knew I was getting way too soft and I needed to get back to being a reporter.

Horst came out passing, using the whole field and all his receivers. He gained nine yards on a slant to the tight end, twenty-four on a post pattern to a wide-out, twelve on a pass into the flat. Before Ferris could get set, Horst hurried the team to the line, faked a handoff to Shawn Warner, and gained another eleven on a naked bootleg. Ferris was reeling, and Horst didn't give them a chance to breathe. From the shotgun he threw a bomb down the sideline for Lenny Westwood, who was streaking toward the end zone. Westwood went up for the ball with a Ferris defender right with him. For an instant they both had it, but then the Ferris guy took the ball away, just out-muscled Westwood. Around me, everyone groaned in disbelief, while on the other side of the dome Ferris's fans screamed for joy.

I typed a one-sentence description of the play, got the Ferris guy's number so I could find his name later, and then looked down at the field to see our defense racing onto the field. Would it be Clarke at middle linebacker? No—there was Angel Marichal, right in the middle, right where he'd belonged all year. McNulty wasn't hiding him anymore.

Ferris had lived by pounding the ball right at defenses, so that's what McNulty was expecting. He had Angel crowding the line, bird-dogging Micah Pengilly. But on first down Ferris's quarterback faked a handoff to Pengilly and hit a little quick screen in the flat that went for twelve. Ferris's second play was a carbon copy of the first—another dump-off pass for another first down. Angel backed off the line to protect against the pass and—*boom*—Pengilly sliced through the defense for twenty-one yards. Worse, the guy who finally hauled him down drew a facemask penalty.

Now, deep in our territory, Ferris did pound the ball. The PA announcer sounded like a broken record: *Micah Pengilly for seven yards; Micah Pengilly for six yards; Micah Pengilly into the end zone for a touchdown.*

As Pengilly celebrated with his teammates along their sideline, I typed furiously, trying to capture in words what I'd just seen. At no time in the season had a team cut through the Lincoln defense quite the way Ferris had. Play after play I kept thinking: *This time Angel will do something.* But the Ferris offensive line had pushed our guys around as if they were a JV team. Ferris was likely to score, and score often.

For Lincoln to have a chance, Horst needed to put up points, and on the second possession he came out firing again. He threw an incompletion on first down, but then clicked on two straight bullets to his old friend Lenny Westwood. After that, Shawn Warner busted up the gut for thirteen yards. Next it was an end-around for thirty-four. After each play, Horst pushed the tempo, never letting Ferris get set. And they weren't set on the last play of the drive—a feathery pass to Westwood, who took it in at the five and waltzed into the end zone.

Ferris 7, Lincoln 7.

Pengilly was the deep man on kickoff (did the guy do everything?) and he took the ball out to the forty. I was expecting another long march the length of the field. Why not? Both offenses seemed way ahead of the defenses. But on this drive, our linemen held their ground against the O-line of Ferris. Angel stuffed Pengilly after a gain of two yards on first down and actually dropped him for a loss on second down. That made third down an obvious passing down. Angel blitzed, the Ferris QB hurried his throw, and the ball sailed out of bounds. Ferris had to kick—the first punt of the game—and the Lincoln fans around me cheered in appreciation.

Stein took the short kick and brought it back to the Lincoln forty, and out came Horst again. If you'd been living in outer space, and you showed up at the game, and someone said, "Who do you think the best player out there is?" you'd have pointed to Horst and said, "He is." He was so calm, as if the game were in slow motion, yet somehow he was playing faster than anyone. First play: nineteen yards on an out pattern. Second play: quarterback draw for nine. Third play: screen pass to Warner for fourteen more. Fourth play: another pass to Westwood, with an unnecessary roughness penalty tacked on at the end, bringing the ball to the Ferris four. It took Warner three tries, but on the last play of the first quarter he punched the ball in.

Lincoln 14, Ferris 7.

All through the first quarter, nearly everything had clicked for both offenses. In the second, nothing did. The defenses didn't stop the offenses—Angel was still struggling because of the strength of the Ferris offensive line. The offenses stopped themselves with penalties or dropped passes or botched plays. What had been a crisply played game turned into a sloppy mess.

With less than two minutes left before halftime, Horst hit Shawn Warner on a screen pass. Warner needed two yards for the first, and if he'd just plunged straight ahead, he'd have had them. Instead he stopped, doubled back, then doubled back again, and was finally dropped for a seventeen-yard loss. McNulty went berserk on the sideline, slamming his clipboard to the ground. A first down would have meant Lincoln could have run out the clock. Now McNulty had no choice but to punt.

It was a good punt—too good. Pengilly had to back up ten yards to catch it, but that gave him ten yards of open field. He broke right, reversed, and came back left, picking up a wall of blockers. Kenstowicz, the punter, had the last shot to stop him, which was no shot at all. Pengilly gave him a little stutter step and then blew right by him. Sixty-four yards and a touchdown. McNulty glared at Warner and then flung his clipboard to the ground again. At the half the score was Ferris 14, Lincoln 14.

The Lincoln band marched onto the field as the players headed to the locker room. I wanted to stay right where I was, but I had to go out to the parking lot. "If you leave you can't come back," an usher said as I approached the exit where he was stationed.

"I've got a press pass," I said, flashing my badge.

He looked confused for a moment, and then shrugged. "All right, I guess that makes it different. It's raining out there, though."

"That's okay. I'm burning up."

And I was. My face was on fire and I felt myself sweating. Would the Civic be there? I stepped outside. The rain felt good on my face, and so did the cold. I looked out toward the back fence of the half-filled South lot. Was that a car? I stared long and hard, but it was too dark to know for sure.

12

IT WAS STRANGE HEADING BACK into the Tacoma Dome for the second half. All the banners, all the cheers, all the excited voices—it didn't seem possible that the world of color and light inside the dome was the same world that might be hiding a black Civic in a dark parking lot by a battered fence.

I returned to my seat, opened my laptop, and looked onto the field. The players from both teams were jumping up and down on the sidelines, pumping themselves up for the second half, butting helmets the same way rams butt horns.

Ferris had the first possession of the second half. They came out doing what had gotten them to the finals— putting the ball in Micah Pengilly's hands. First it was a screen pass for a dozen yards; then a toss sweep for six more followed by a quick-hitter up the middle for yet another first down. Angel was getting more than his share of tackles, but none of them were in the backfield for losses, or even at the line of scrimmage. The Ferris guys were again dominating the game up-front, pushing the Lincoln guys around.

On second and two from the Lincoln nineteen, Pengilly cut back against the grain, was hit hard by a cornerback, and went down awkwardly. The Ferris trainer came out, talked to him a bit, and then he limped off to applause from both sides.

With Pengilly on the sideline, McNulty figured Ferris would pass, so he sent Angel on a blitz right over the center. The Ferris QB saw Angel coming and unloaded the ball just before Angel nailed him. The hit looked perfectly okay to me and to every other Lincoln fan, but a yellow flag fluttered to the ground. *"Personal foul—roughing the passer . . . half the distance to the goal line."*

On first down from the nine, Angel blitzed again, but this time the fullback picked him up. The quarterback, with all the time in the world, found a wide receiver in the back of the end zone.

Ferris 21, Lincoln 14.

It was only one touchdown, but I could feel the anxiety around me. Except for one series in the first half, Ferris's front line had manhandled our guys. Now they'd scored *without* Pengilly on the field. Along the sideline Pengilly was running ten-yard wind sprints. He was coming back. Were they simply the better team?

After the kickoff, McNulty didn't go for the quick strike, choosing instead to run the ball with Shawn Warner, mixing in a few short passes to keep the defense honest. Horst moved the team downfield while, along the sideline, Lincoln's defensive coaches had that unit together, coaching them on the fly. Our drive stalled after a holding call, but Kenstowicz came on and delivered a thirty-four yard field goal to cut the lead to 21–17.

The defense had had plenty of time to rest, and they'd had a quick lesson, but neither did any good. It was Pengilly left, Pengilly right, Pengilly, Pengilly, Pengilly. Angel kept fighting, but it was as if he were running up a muddy hill that four guys were charging down. Ferris kept gaining yards, the game clock kept ticking, and Angel was wearing down.

They were on our twenty when the third quarter ended, and they ran off six more plays and used three minutes of the fourth quarter before they scored on a one-yard quarterback sneak.

Ferris 28, Lincoln 17.

When Horst returned, he was facing the biggest challenge of the season. He was down two scores, and all the momentum was on Ferris's side. The big-time college recruiters would be judging him on this moment—Horst had to know that.

And yet, to look at him, you'd have thought he was playing ball in his backyard with some buddies. He trotted onto the field, helmet in hand, a smile on his face. He patted Warner on the back, rubbed his hands together, pulled his helmet on, and then leaned into the huddle to call the play just as he'd called plays all year long.

With an eleven-point lead, Ferris changed their defense, dropping their safeties deep, trying to take away the deep threat and the quick touchdown. That left the underneath routes open, so that's what Horst took. Passes in the flat, passes over the middle, quick outs. Five yards, eight yards, seven yards. Lincoln was collecting first down after first down. It would have been a great drive except for one thing—the clock. The seconds kept ticking away, and with every tick, Ferris moved closer to the state title.

On a second and six from the Ferris thirty, Horst dropped back to pass. No one was open, and he was flushed out of the pocket. He kept pumping his arm as if he was going to throw. At the last second he tucked the ball under his arm and turned upfield.

A Ferris safety closed on him. He was expecting Horst to go down, but Horst lowered his shoulder and bowled the safety over, the way he'd done so many times before. He made it inside the ten before he was gang tackled. On the next play, with the Lincoln fans roaring, Horst found

Shawn Warner leaking out of the backfield. Warner caught the ball in stride at the three and bulled his way in for the score.

That touchdown made the score 28–23 and made a two-point conversion attempt a no-brainer. Horst took the snap, faked a quick pass to Westwood on the left, and then spun and handed the ball to Warner coming the other way. The Ferris defenders had gone for the fake. Warner could have walked in, but he fumbled the handoff. He ran, hands down, trying to scoop it up, but it kept bounding away. Finally a Ferris guy hit him and another Ferris guy fell on the ball, and the score stayed 28–23.

I looked at the clock. Four minutes and four seconds left, and now a field goal would be meaningless; Lincoln had to get the ball back and score a touchdown.

Ferris had seven guys up expecting an onside kick, but Kenstowicz knuckled an in-between sort of kick that landed at the thirty-five, bounced left, and then kicked right. Angel was one of the guys racing down trying to recover it. I thought he'd do it, too; I'd seen him make so many great plays, but at the bottom of the pile was a Ferris guy.

Horst had burned one time-out early in the third quarter, so Lincoln had two left. The math was pretty simple. If

Ferris got a first down, they'd be able to run out the clock. Horst had done his job; now it was the defense's turn, Angel's turn. Everyone in the stadium was up, and everyone knew what was coming.

Micah Pengilly.

The Ferris quarterback took the snap and made a quick pitch. Pengilly took it wide left, then cut back. Angel swatted at the ball, trying to force a fumble, but Pengilly hung on, falling forward for a three-yard gain. McNulty used his second time-out. Three forty-seven left.

On second down Ferris came right up the middle. All game their offensive line had blown our defensive line back, but this time the line held. Pengilly squeezed forward for one paltry yard before he was hauled down. Immediately McNulty burned his final time-out. Three thirty-eight.

Third down and six yards for a first down. Would Ferris pass? If they did, they'd have a good chance for a completion since both safeties were cheating forward. But an incompletion would stop the clock, and that was the last thing Ferris wanted to do.

Angel was hopping up and backing away, trying to confuse the quarterback. The quarterback took the snap and dropped back to pass. Our defensive line broke past the blockers—and then I saw it. A screen pass—a safe pass—

to Pengilly. He caught it with two blockers in front. He looked certain to gain enough for the first down. Angel had shed the first blocker, but the second guy hit him from the side. As Angel went down, he reached out his hand and caught Pengilly's foot. Pengilly staggered, almost regained his balance, but then one knee touched the ground—two yards short of a first down. Lincoln would get the ball back.

McNulty had no time-outs left, so Ferris let the play clock wind down to *one* before snapping the ball. Their punter got off a great kick, a high booming spiral. Stein turned left, then turned right, and then just got out of the way. The ball rolled and rolled, inside the thirty, inside the twenty-five, eating seconds off the clock. Finally it rolled dead on the twenty-three.

Two minutes and forty-four seconds remained. Lincoln was seventy-seven yards from the end zone and had no time-outs left.

Horst brought the offense out onto the field. Ferris was in their prevent defense again, making it impossible for Horst to go long with anything, forcing him to dump the ball over the middle.

The receivers tried to make the catch and then fight their way out of bounds to stop the clock, but the Ferris guys would keep them in bounds and so keep the clock moving. We were driving, but even though Horst was running a no-huddle offense, it was all happening too slowly. A first down on our thirty-five with 1:50 on the clock. A first down at our forty-seven with 0:59 left on the clock. A first down at their forty-six with 0:37 left.

That's when we got lucky. A Ferris player went down clutching his leg, his head bobbing from left to right in pain. The crowd, which had been screaming with every play, went quiet. The Ferris trainer came out and starting working on his calf. A cramp—painful, but not serious. And in the time that the trainer took to get him up and off the field, McNulty had huddled with his offense. There was time for three or four plays, but no more. Five yards a crack wasn't going to make it; something big had to happen.

When play resumed, Horst was in the shotgun. He took the snap, faked a quick outlet pass to Westwood on the right, and then went for the long bomb to Price streaking down the left side toward the end zone. For an instant it seemed he was in the clear, but then Ferris's safety rotated over to knock the ball away.

Second down and ten. Twenty-nine seconds left.

Again Horst was in the shotgun; again he used play-action, this time a fake draw to Shawn Warner. He was looking for Westwood on a post pattern, but the Ferris middle linebacker had dropped into coverage. He put his big hand up and deflected the pass, nearly pulling off the interception. The Ferris side went wild with joy; on Lincoln's side, everyone groaned.

Third and ten. Twenty-one seconds remaining.

Horst took the snap, pump-faked another long pass, and then fired a bullet to a wide receiver running an out pattern. The receiver caught the ball at the thirty-five but backtracked to get out of bounds to stop the clock. The refs brought the chains out and measured—he was short of a first down by six inches.

Fourth down. Twelve seconds on the clock. Thirty-seven yards from the end zone.

What do you do? Go for the quick first down on another out pattern and then take a final shot at the end zone? Or take the final shot right now?

I was so tense that I almost didn't see Angel come in at wide receiver. When I did spot him, I sensed what was coming, and my breathing stopped, and I didn't hear the roar around me.

Horst took the snap and stepped back. He turned and quickly fired a pass to Angel in the flat. Only it wasn't a pass. Angel had retreated three steps from the line of scrimmage, turning Horst's bullet into a lateral. The cornerback was closing on Angel, lining him up for the game-ending tackle. But Angel cocked his right arm, and it was as if I were back on Gilman Field in August watching him for the first time. The ball was out of his hand in a split second, a laser beam down the sideline for the streaking Lenny Westwood.

Ferris's safety was just a yard behind Westwood, but Angel's pass was so pure that all Westwood needed was a foot. For the briefest instant, Westwood bobbled the ball, but then he pulled it in, and a moment later he was crossing the goal line, Angel was being swarmed by his teammates, Lincoln was the state champion, the people around me were going crazy with joy, and I was going crazy too.

THE LINCOLN BAND MARCHED onto the field as the players jumped on one another and then raced over to the Lincoln side of the dome and jumped up and down in front of their parents and their classmates.

The PA announcer directed everyone's attention to midfield, where the trophy was presented to Coach McNulty. Kimi snapped pictures as McNulty raised the trophy over his head and then handed it to Horst, who did the same. People cheered each time, but each time the volume decreased. Ten minutes after the game ended, barely half of Lincoln's fans remained in the stands, and with every second more were leaving. Ten minutes later the team was leaving, heading to the locker room. They'd celebrate among themselves for a while, but soon Angel would take the long walk to the parking lot, bright lights overhead, concrete on all sides.

I headed out into the night. Instead of going down the ramps to the parking lot, I went to the railing and looked out. The rain had stopped, yet the night had grown colder. Cars were jammed up at the exits, but even as I watched, traffic started to loosen. Soon there'd be no line at all.

I turned my eyes to the back fence—still too dark to know for sure. And then I saw a sudden flash of light in the darkness. What was it? I looked harder. A match—it had to be a match. A moment later it went out, but then another one was lit, and now I could see the red glow of the lit end of two cigarettes.

They were there, right where I thought they'd be. Two of them sitting in the Civic, smoking, waiting for the parking lot to empty, waiting for their chance.

I took out my cell phone and called Kimi. "Where are you?"

"By the players' gate."

"Are there any police cars there or security guys?"

"Let me look." A pause, and then she came back on the line. "I don't see any."

"Kimi, if I don't call you back within the next fifteen minutes, get away from there."

"What?"

"You heard me. Get away from there."

"Is the Civic here? Did you find it? I could call the police."

"Do it. Call the police. Tell them to get somebody at the players' gate."

"What are you going to do?"

"If I don't call back," I repeated, "get away from there. Even if the police show up. You've got to promise."

"Okay. I promise. What are you going to do now?"

"There's no time to explain." Before she could reply, I closed up my phone and turned it off.

I'd reached this moment in my mind many times. Each time I'd wondered if I'd have the necessary courage. Now that I was finally here in the flesh, it was as if I were somehow out of my own body, as if the real me were watching this other me—this brave me—watching him in amazement, because even though the other me was afraid, he didn't let the fear stop him.

I walked to where the Focus was parked. I put the laptop in the trunk, and took the hunting knife out from the pouch. I had to be fast, and yet not rush.

I zigzagged through the parking lot until I reached a spot by the back fence that was one hundred yards east of the Civic. I crouched low and slowly moved toward it, retracing the steps I'd taken hours earlier. Seventy-five yards . . . fifty yards . . . forty . . . thirty.

At about twenty yards I could both hear and feel the deep bass of a super-loud sound system. The guys in the car were listening to some rap CD, probably psyching themselves up for the craziness they were planning. It was a break for me—they wouldn't hear my footsteps on the gravel. At fifteen yards, I dropped to my knees and inched along, careful to stay low. Ten yards . . . five yards, and then, finally, I was there.

All I'd done was creep along a fence for one hundred yards, but I was drenched in sweat. I stayed still for a minute, letting my heart slow, before reaching into my back pocket and pulling out the knife. I unsheathed it and fingered the razor-sharp blade.

That's when the passenger door of the Civic opened.

Music spilled out, and so did a thin layer of light. I sprawled face-down into the gravel. The driver's door opened next. I slithered under the car, the gravel biting into my hands and arms and face. I was sure I was making noise, but the crazy-loud volume of the car stereo saved me.

I couldn't see them, but I could see their feet. They'd moved to the front of the car and were looking toward the Tacoma Dome. Were they going to move now? Was I too late?

They were talking, but I couldn't make out anything they were saying. Then one of them dropped a cigarette to the ground right by his foot and started walking toward the back of the car. I pressed myself deeper into the ground; my breathing stopped.

I watched his feet until he drew even with my face, but I didn't dare turn my head to follow his progress after that. Instead, I lay perfectly still. The footsteps stopped and a moment later I heard the hatchback door open, heard the guy fumbling around for something. He must have found it—whatever it was—because a second later he slammed the hatchback door shut. I flinched—it had sounded like a gunshot. But now the guy was moving again. He moved away from the back of the Civic up to the passenger door, opened it, and sat down. The driver got back in the car as well, and I listened to one door slam shut and then the other.

The added weight caused the carriage of the car to drop down an inch or two. That doesn't sound like much, but I had hardly any clearance before. I was terrified; I had a knife in my hand, two killers sitting not five feet from me. I wriggled like an eel to get out from under the Civic, the whole time thanking God that I'd lost weight. If I hadn't, I might have been stuck there, helpless.

Gravel was embedding itself into my forearms, and my pant legs were riding up, but finally I cleared the bumper. It was time. From a kneeling position, I ran my hand over the back passenger tire, feeling for a spot between the knobby tread. I found one, and pushed with the knife. The rubber didn't give. I fought down the panic. I pushed again. Still the rubber didn't give. I'd come this far—I couldn't fail. I brought the knife back one more time and then shoved the blade as hard as I could into the tire. For an instant the rubber resisted, but then it gave way.

The blade was in.

I left it there for a long moment before slowly working it out, rocking the blade back and forth to increase the size of the puncture. When the blade came clear, I heard a loud hissing sound. It sounded like a jet taking off to me. I expected the car doors to open and the guys to jump out and start beating on me, but then I felt the deep bass of the CD player, and I knew they'd heard nothing.

I listened to the escaping air until I was certain the tire was going flat. Only then did I start back along the fence line, first creeping on my hands and knees and then later crouching low as I walked. When I was one hundred yards away, I wiped the dirt off my hands and my shirt and my pants as best I could, and headed back toward the T-Dome.

I was sky-high as I walked out of the dark and into the light, so high I wanted to scream for pure joy. By the time I reached the dome the tire would be down on the rim. The moment those guys started the car up and tried to drive forward, they'd feel it for sure. The flat tire ended everything. No way were they flying up to the players' gate and firing shots and then racing off on Interstate 5. When Angel came down the walkway, they'd have the trunk up and they'd be looking at their silly undersize spare tire. After they changed the tire—if they knew how—they'd be poking along the frontage road at thirty-five miles an hour while Angel was headed . . . where?

It didn't matter where.

He'd be long gone, off to some place that only McNulty would know.

I tossed the knife into a garbage can, took out my cell phone, turned it back on, and called Kimi.

"The police haven't come," she said, frantic.

"It doesn't matter. There's nothing to worry about anymore. I'll be there in a few minutes."

By the time I reached her, the first players were coming out of the locker room and were heading down the walkway leading into the parking lot. They came in groups of five and six, and they were quieter than I thought they'd be. The game and the trophy presentation and the time in the locker room had worn them out. Kimi took pictures as they passed, and Horst stopped and posed. "Did you get me holding the trophy?" he asked, and when Kimi said she had, he smiled. The last two out were McNulty and Angel. Kimi had her camera up to her eye, but when she recognized them, she put the lens cap on and let the camera hang around her neck.

I nodded as they reached us. McNulty looked at me, but he made no acknowledgment. Angel didn't even look. As they passed, I saw the cousin waiting at the end of the chute. McNulty and Angel shook hands, a handshake of goodbye. Angel got in his cousin's car, and they drove off.

"So that's that," Kimi said.

"Yeah," I said. "That's that."

We walked to the other side of the dome where the Focus was parked. I had an odd feeling that it wouldn't start, but it did. I followed the orange cones to the exit. As I left the parking lot, I looked over to the back fence. The hatchback of the Civic was up, the light just bright enough for me to see two guys staring down into it.

"So the Civic wasn't there?" Kimi said when we were out on the freeway.

"It was there," I said.

"Then why were you so sure everything was so safe?"

I looked over at her. "Because I slashed their tire."

"What?"

I grinned. "I slashed their tire. Rear passenger tire, to be precise. Rocked the knife back and forth until I was sure I'd put a huge hole in it."

Her eyes were wide in disbelief. "You're making this up."

"No, I'm not."

"Show me the knife."

"I threw it away."

"Why?"

"Why not? I'm not going to make a career of slashing tires."

When we reached Seattle, we went to the Fremont Peet's. We sat upstairs and Kimi asked me over and over to describe how I'd slashed the tire of the Civic. It was the scrapes and cuts I'd gotten from the gravel that finally convinced her.

"That was really brave," she said, but then a little smile came to her face.

"What?" I said.

"Nothing."

"Tell me."

She shrugged. "We never saw a gun or anything, so we'll never know for sure that they were coming after Angel. They might have been there for some completely normal reason." She paused, and then reached over and put her hand on top of mine. "Don't get me wrong, Mitch. You were really, really courageous. But you see what I mean, don't you?"

I nodded. "Yeah, I see what you mean."

I drove her home. "Are you going to take photos during basketball season?" I asked when I pulled up in front of her house.

"I don't know. I've got AP tests to study for."

"AP tests aren't until May."

She opened the car door and stepped out. "I'll probably take photos," she said, and I knew right then that she wouldn't. I waited until she was inside her house before pulling away from the curb and heading home.

We'll never know for sure that they were coming after Angel.

As I'd been crawling along the fence, as I'd been hiding under the car, as I'd been plunging the knife into the tire—the whole time I'd known deep down that the guys in the Civic might be there for any of a thousand reasons. Maybe I'd been a hero, but maybe I'd been a vandal.

I turned onto my block and eased the Focus into the driveway. After I switched off the engine, I stayed in the car for a moment, too tired even to open the door, every muscle sapped of strength. After a minute I stepped out, locked the Focus, and started toward my house.

They appeared out of the darkness. There were two guys, both dressed in black, both bigger than I was. "You Mitch True," one of them hissed.

"What?" I said.

"You heard me."

"Yeah, I'm Mitch True."

He buried his fist into my stomach.

"Where's he live?" His voice was low but threatening.

"Wh-who?" I stammered, feeling the taste of vomit in my mouth.

"Don't mess with us. Angel Delarosa or Marichal or whatever he calls himself. Where's he live?"

"I don't know what you're talking about."

"Yes, you do, you piece of crap." And then there was another fist, and another one. "We'll beat it out of you if we have to. Where's he live?"

"I don't know." I said, gasping.

I was bent three quarters of the way over, hunched in on myself. Mucus was coming out of my nose and my ears were roaring. I coughed, and phlegm mixed with vomit came up.

The guy stepped back. "You puked on me," he hissed, and then he hit me on the back of the head. I fell to the ground.

"Where's he live?"

"I don't know."

And then they were kicking me, both of them, kicking me and kicking me, saying I'd better tell them. I couldn't have answered even if I'd wanted to, because a blackness was coming at me, a deep inky blackness was coming to swallow me, and then it did swallow me, and I was glad to be swallowed.

I don't know how long I was out, but the next thing I remember is Big Red, Mrs. Marilley's dog, standing over me, his long wet tongue making repeated visits to my mouth, my cheek, my eyes. I moaned, and that made Big Red whimper. "Good boy," I said, and I managed to sit up. He backed up, doing a little tap dance on the sidewalk, and then he started barking at me. "It's okay," I said. "Shhh."

I struggled to my knees and then to my feet and took a few wobbly steps toward my front door. Big Red made a crazy leap, barked once, and then ran off—no doubt to poop on somebody's lawn.

I managed to open the front door, climb upstairs to my room, stagger into the bathroom, and turn on the shower. The hot water hurt and felt great at the same time. I let it cascade over me for a long time. When I'd washed away all the snot and puke, I dried myself, put on my robe, and fell onto my bed. I lay there, the world spinning, for a long, long time.

And then, in a flash, I realized what had happened, and exactly what it meant. My head was roaring from pain and my guts felt like somebody had put them in a blender, but I've never felt better than I did at that moment. And I don't think I ever will.

EPILOGUE

WHEN MY DAD SAW ME the next morning, he knew immediately I'd been in a fight. I told him that some Ferris guys had followed me home after the game and had beaten me up. "Why you?" he asked.

"I guess maybe they figured out I was a reporter."

"That makes no sense at all," my mother said, her eyes welling up with tears. "No sense at all."

My parents drove me to the emergency room. "Concussion," the doctor said, "and severely bruised ribs. Don't be surprised if you have headaches. A week home, minimum." It was Thanksgiving week—not a bad week to miss. I wouldn't have to make up too much homework.

When we left the hospital, my dad wanted to take me to the police station to file a report, but I talked him out of it. "I didn't get a good look at them. I'd never be able to recognize them."

That part was true. Even the time at school when they'd jumped out of the Civic, I'd been so scared I hadn't really *seen* them.

Kimi called Monday when I didn't show up at school. I'd thought about keeping what had happened secret, the way Clint Eastwood might. Clint would know what he'd done, and that would be all that mattered to him.

But I'm not Clint Eastwood. After I finished telling Kimi everything, she insisted on coming to my house to see me. She arrived around four. As soon as she stepped inside, she hugged me tight, told me how brave I'd been, and kissed me on the cheek. It was the way a sister kisses her brother—again—but that was okay. We drank a cup of tea in the kitchen, and I told her everything for a second and then a third time. Around five the doorbell rang. "That's Marianne," she said. "We're going over to Erica's to watch a movie." I walked her to the door and she hugged me for what I was sure was the last time.

Only it wasn't. The day I returned to school, she asked me to go to the Winter Ball with her. "Not with me alone," she added quickly. "There will be about twenty of us. We'll rent a stretch limousine. It'll be fun."

When the night finally arrived I was nervous, but the limousine and the twenty other people made it better. I danced with Kimi once and we had our picture taken together, but she spent ninety-nine percent of the time with Rachel and Marianne. I wandered around talking to this person and that. Around midnight I found myself standing next to a girl who went to Roosevelt High. We talked awhile, and it turned out she was the starting softball pitcher there. I told her I was the sports reporter for the *Lincoln Light* and that I'd see her pitch in the spring.

"Make sure you wave to me," she said.

I liked talking to her, and she seemed to like talking to me, because she didn't look around for her date, whoever he was. I would have kept talking to Amy, but Kimi came over and said that we were all leaving. If I'd been thinking, I'd have gotten Amy's phone number.

College letters came in the spring. The thick manila envelopes were good news, the thin white ones bad; but good or bad they arrived addressed to Daniel True. I liked seeing that name. It's too late to try to change things at Lincoln, but I'm through with being Mitch.

Columbia was a thin envelope, which was actually a relief. I've lost all desire to go to any place with mean streets. I did get into a little college in Kentucky that's supposed to be great. I don't know why I applied there, but now I'm thinking I might actually go. I still plan on making a name for myself as a reporter, but I'm not in a hurry anymore. Being out in the middle of nowhere, reading books, and learning things—that doesn't sound like a bad way to spend four years.

Kimi got into Cornell, which isn't Princeton, but which is an Ivy League school, so she's happy. She says she wants to keep in touch and that maybe we could even visit each other over spring break.

I gained some weight back over Christmas, but since then I've been losing steadily, though slowly. I do my same run, across the footbridge to Magnolia. Every once in a while I veer off to Elmore Street. Whenever I run by Angel's house, I try to picture just where he disappeared to after the game, and what he's doing now. When my mind really gets going, I try to imagine what his entire future will be like. I've thought about it so much that I've actually worked it all out.

So here's Angel's life, according to me:

After the championship game, he and his cousin drive up to Canada. McNulty knows a coach up there, and Angel ends up with a football scholarship at the University of British Columbia. He has to take another new name, and he grows a goatee and shaves his head, but he's still the same phenomenal player on the field. He plays four years at middle linebacker at UBC, leading his team in tackles every year. After college, he's drafted in the second round by the Toronto Argonauts. He makes a bundle of money in the CFL, meets a French-speaking girl on the road, marries her, has two boys, and ends up living on a quiet, tree-lined street in Montreal.

Nobody from Philadelphia ever bothers him again.